THE
KNIGHTS

Stuka Squadron Series
Book One

Charles Whiting
writing as
Leo Kessler

SAPERE
BOOKS

Also in the Stuka Squadron Series
Hawks of Death
Tank-busters
Blood Mission

THE BLACK KNIGHTS

Published by Sapere Books.

24 Trafalgar Road, Ilkley, LS29 8HH

saperebooks.com

ISBN: 978-0-85495-227-4

BOOK 1: *THE BLACK KNIGHTS GO TO WAR*

CHAPTER 1

'*Achtung, meine Herren-sie kommen!*'

The harsh metallic voice echoed and re-echoed suddenly the whole length of the bombing range. As one, all eyes turned to the west. Binoculars swung upwards. Hurriedly the elegant staff officers grouped around *Reichsmarschall* Göring and *General der SS* Himmler adjusted them. Silently the tight group of sinister black dots eased into the gleaming circles of calibrated glass.

The observers were hard, realistic, even brutal men, but here and there one of them licked his lips nervously; for there seemed something uncanny, even a little frightening, about this new weapon which the Führer had already confidently predicted would win the war in the West for the Reich. 'The lead plane,' the loudspeaker burst into harsh life once more, 'is a fighter commanded by Major Greim, who is the C.O. of the First SS Stuka Squadron.' Himmler smirked at the mention, Göring frowned and ran the handful of uncut diamonds he clutched in his beringed, pudgy fingers through them like a Greek his worry beads. 'You can see him zig-zagging about his squadron to give it fighter protection against attack at the crucial moment. Now his squadron comes in … in flights of four.'

In their glasses the observers could now see the black sinister gull-winged planes with their gaping radiators and slender undercarriage legs, and on their sleek sides the silver emblem of the SS surmounted by the helmet insignia of the 'Black Knights'.

'The first flight is commanded by *Untersturmbannführer der SS* Baron Karst... The second by *Untersturmbannführer der* SS Furst Schwarz...'

'God in heaven,' Göring, the head of the German Air Force, cursed, his berouged face flushing an even deeper red, his perfumed jowls wobbling with rage, 'do we have to have all these shit-damned SS ranks!'

Next to him, Himmler smiled, his pale schoolteacher's face full of pride. 'My dear Göring, do not begrudge us of the SS one single squadron of Stuka pilots when you of the *Luftwaffe* have whole wings of them,' he said mildly, fussing with his gold-rimmed pince-nez.

Göring lowered his binoculars for an instant. He wagged a lacquered nail under Himmler's nose, trembling with suppressed rage, while the two men's staffs waited apprehensively for the outburst to come. 'In three devils' name, Himmler, you know as well as I do that I have opposed the establishment of the First SS Stuka Squadron right from the start ever since you put that particular flea in the Führer's ear!' he bellowed, spittle flecking the corners of his lips, coloured a bold carmine-red with lipstick. 'I, Reichsmarshal Göring, am the head of Germany's Air Force and I demand —'

'— *THEY ATTACK* —' the excited bellow of the commentator cut into the fat Marshal's angry outburst. '*THEY ATTACK — NOW ... THE STUKAS ARE COMING!*'

Major Greim flung an anxious look at Karst to his right. Harshly handsome, dour and ambitious, Baron Karst was a man, he knew, who would take impossible risks this day to impress his beloved *Reichsführer* SS Heinrich Himmler. He hoped in God's name that the Baron would hit his air brakes in time and pull out; in these last months of training for the campaign to come in the West there had been only too many Stuka pilots who had forgotten to do that in the tremendous exhilarating, almost sexual, excitement of the dive. The ground crews had been forced to scrape the remains from the ground. He waggled his wings. Karst nodded and pulled down his goggles with a slow deliberate movement. Behind him his gunner Hanneman, a sergeant of the regular *Luftwaffe*, crossed himself with mock solemnity, and did the same. Greim grinned momentarily. Sergeant Hanneman, the squadron's most notorious skirt-chaser and boozer, was a card.

Karst waggled his wings. Around him his flight seemed to be hovering in mid-air like sinister black metal hawks. He took a deep breath. '*Now!*' he cried, taking one last haughty arrogant look at his Black Knights, and pushed her over.

The Stuka seemed to fall out of the bright blue spring sky. Sirens screaming, it hurtled towards the white circle of the target set in the green of the grass field, at a crazy impossible speed. One hundred kilometres … two hundred … three hundred kilometres … four hundred… Karst, controlled in his cold dour way, yet excited beyond all measure underneath, checked his flickering green instruments as the ground rushed up to meet him. *6,000 … 5,400 … 5,100 … 4,800 … 4,500 … 1,000 metres* … they were screaming towards the target at a tremendous rate, the whole plane creaking and shrieking under the pressure. Karst gasped for breath. The blood pounded at his temples. A veil of red spread over his eyes. He felt his bones twisting under the pressure. His guts seemed about to burst. His cheekbones squeezed at his eye-sockets. Hard cruel fingers pressed deep into his eye balls. Blood started to stream from his nostrils and ears. The white circle loomed ever larger.

'Holy strawsack!' Hanneman shrieked in a paroxysm of fear, awe and excitement as the ground zoomed up at an impossible speed. 'Drop the shitting thing ... *drop the egg* ... NOW!'

Karst fought back the black mist which was threatening to overcome him. He hit the rudder bar hard and pressed the toggle at the same moment. '*Sieg Heil!*' he screamed in ecstasy. With all his strength he heaved at the stick. His eyes bulged out of his head like those of a madman. Sweat streamed down his face under the leather helmet. For an instant his sight blurred red. Momentarily he blacked out under that tremendous pressure, pinned against the back of his seat, his guts seemingly slammed against his spine by the centrifugal force. Then he was soaring high into the bright blue, while his flight hurtled down behind him and his own bomb headed straight for the centre of the white circle.

'*Großartig!*' Himmler exclaimed, as the bomb exploded. A thunderclap. A flash of flame and a wet searing slap of blast in the face for the observers. 'What do you say to my Black Knights now, Göring, eh?' The head of the SS stamped his right foot down excitedly like a petulant child.

'Aren't they the best?'

Göring swallowed hard, his eardrums seared by the howl of air-brakes, the shriek of the Stukas' sirens and the slap of the bombs exploding dead on target. His faded blue eyes were cold and listless and without enthusiasm, although he knew Greim had trained his aristocrats of the SS up to the standard of his best regular *Luftwaffe* pilots. He knew what Himmler was after. As always he was trying to expand his personal empire. The Stukas, his 'flying artillery', as he would often call them, would be at the forefront of the battle to come in the West. The Stukas would win all the glory of the victory that the Führer confidently expected, and Himmler wanted some of that glory for his SS — urgently. 'They are quite good,' he said carefully, realizing suddenly he needed a shot of that cunning white powder; his energy was fading rapidly, 'quite good.'

'*Quite good!*' Himmler's sickly pale face flushed hotly, 'why my dear Reichsmarshal, every one of those bombs so far has landed directly on the target! That is precision bombing of the highest order. My —'

'— Third flight coming in now,' the loud metallic voice cut into his angry protest, 'commanded by *Untersturmbannführer* de la Mazière!… *Here they come, meine Herren!*'

The last flight fell out of the sky like a string of black pearls. Sirens howled ear-splittingly. Coming in at a 90 degree angle, flinging themselves defiantly at the earth, their motors wailing like banshees, the Stukas raced to the attack at four hundred kilometres an hour.

De la Mazière, lean, tough and bronzed, watched as the target hurtled up towards him. Behind him his air-gunner 'Slack Arse' Schmidt tensed. He knew his commander. He was fair and decent — for an SS officer — towards the *Luftwaffe* other ranks — 'the peasants', as they called themselves sullenly, but he was a Prussian, too: the descendant of a long-line of soldiers, whose first duty had always been to the state. Officers like that, he told himself as the target loomed up ever larger, the white now pitted brown everywhere like the work of a giant mole, could get yer deaded right smartish.

De la Mazière tensed. Before him on the controls the green needles were oscillating crazily. He gasped for breath. A wild excitement surged through his blood. Inside him an urgent little voice cried, '*go on … go on … don't stop now!*' He fought back the almost overwhelming desire to surrender to the forces

10

of atavistic nature and enjoy this wild crazy descent to destruction. He hit the rudder bar and popped the bomb release. For a moment the plane, now freed of the 250 pound bomb, surged forward at an even greater speed. Then de la Mazière hit the brakes and jerked back the joystick. The whole fuselage trembled madly like a wild horse being put to the saddle for the very first time. De la Mazière flung open his mouth. His eardrums were threatening to burst. Red and white stars were popping before his eyes. He gasped for breath like a stranded fish and then he was off, surging high into that beautiful blue sky, free as the air itself. He had done it. His bomb had landed right on target.

High above the range, guiding his Messerschmitt round in a lazy graceful curve, Major Greim breathed a sigh of relief. It was almost over now and none of his Black Knights had pushed their luck too far, thank God! There was only young Ensign von Dorn to go in now and the eighteen-year-old newcomer straight from Flight Training was generally regarded as 'careful within the squadron; behind his back the 'peasants' said the pale-faced, skinny young Ensign was 'downright windy', 'got the draught up his knickers, right and proper!' Greim had heard Hanneman comment cynically more than once. *He* wouldn't do anything foolish.

Now Greim watched, feeling the sweat-soaked stubble of his chin rasp painfully against his leather flying helmet. The Party brass, they contemptuously called 'golden pheasants', had had their demonstration. Soon they would depart and he would be able to have a good stiff shot of *kognak*; he certainly damn well needed it. Suddenly von Dorn flung himself out of the sky. Like a stone plunging to destruction his Stuka hurtled downwards at four hundred kilometres an hour.

Two thousand metres ... one thousand five hundred ... one thousand ... young von Dorn was dead on target, just as professional as his old comrades of the Black Knights. Greim beamed his approval. The greenbeak was doing all right... *Eight hundred metres ... five hundred...* Greim's beam changed to a look of alarm. Von Dorn was rapidly approaching the danger-level... *Four hundred...* Still no sign of him breaking, that fuselage-racking movement that shook the whole plane... *Three hundred...* His dive-brakes were still in position... *Two hundred and fifty...*

'For God's sake,' Greim shrieked helplessly, 'pull her out, man ... *PULL HER OUT!*'...

Too late. At nearly five hundred kilometres an hour, the Stuka slammed into the earth. Nearly eight tons of metal and man hurtled straight into the target circle. A terrifying, tremendous noise. The canopy flew off. The prop buckled and snapped like match wood. With a crash
like thunder, what was left of the Stuka bounced high into the air, scattering crazy flying bits of metal everywhere. Next moment the wreckage had flipped over on its back in a blinding sheet of violent purple flame. A muffled explosion, a burst of white incandescent light and that was that.

Greim pressed the bridge of his nose hard to stop the sudden flow of tears. *Those damned young arrogant aristocrats ... those damn fool fanatics!* The angry words, mixed with compassion, welled up within him. Suddenly feeling exhausted and very old, he turned and setting down the undercarriage, prepared to land, his face abruptly hollowed out to a crimson death's head by the raging fire below.

The Black Knights had had their first casualty of World War Two...

CHAPTER 2

With fat fingers that trembled slightly, Göring spread the white powder on the sheet of paper tacked to Greim's office desk.

Outside the remains of the Stuka still burned fiercely. All around the firemen in their asbestos suits, splattered with molten aluminium, swamped the wreck with carbonic smoke. Here and there they dropped their axes and, overcome by smoke, had to be led away to vomit against the walls, shoulders heaving with the effort, as if they were sobbing heart brokenly.

Greim frowned, his wrinkled craggy face under the shock of greying hair severe. The damned young fool! He had heard what the 'peasants' and the Black Knights had sneered about his courage, and had wanted to prove himself. Now he was dead, a charred shrunken pygmy in that shattered Stuka, the disembowelled engine showing through the copper-red viscera, from which poured thick black smoke, stinking of burning rubber.

Next to him, Göring took a small gold tube, set with rubies that sparkled like a rich Burgundy in the light reflected from the fire, and set it carefully above the powder. One end he now put into his right nostril, pressing the left one closed. Greim shook his head. 'Fat Hermann', as the Black Knights called the grotesque Reichsmarshal contemptuously behind his back, was on coke again. Perhaps he had never been off it since his wound in the old days.

Once Hermann Göring had been his idol, that daring slim young Major whom he had reported to in France in 1918 when Hermann had been the commander of the celebrated Richthofen Squadron: the greatest flying circus on the Western

Front. Then, after the defeat, Hermann had refused to surrender to the victorious allies. Instantly he had fled to exile in Sweden, wounded as he was, and had continued the fight against the *Versaillesdiktat*, that terrible dictated 'Peace' forced on a beaten Germany by the triumphant Amis, Frogs and Tommies.

The enormous Air Force Commander breathed in hard. A large section of the white drug shot up his nostril. He gave a savage almost bestial grunt of pleasure, as if he could already feel its fierce power surging through his bloodstream.

Major Greim's frown deepened. Outside the fire was about beaten. Now he could see a vague shifting crimson glow beneath the boiling white foam. The firemen started to wade into it, axes at the ready, fine powdered aluminium falling on their shoulders in a metallic rain.

Hermann had come a long way since those days in 1918 when he had reported to the Richthofen Squadron as a seventeen-year-old officer-cadet. He had risen to the heights; the Führer's heir he was now, so they said. But he had paid highly for that success. Too much dope, drink and food had turned him into a monster with his painted face and painted nails, changing his uniforms up to twenty times a day. No wonder that his arrogant Black Knights declared contemptuously in the mess that 'Fat Hermann is worth more to the Reich in scrap and lard than he is as a commander!'

Still, Major Greim told himself, as Göring inserted the tube into his other nostril, his fat hands less shaky now, the Reichsmarshal *had* given him his first decent job in twenty years. All that barnstorming in one-horse Mid-Western towns at five dollars a day; risking his neck as a crop-duster in Canada for a dollar, fifty cents an hour; chasing the *Indio* rebels in those God-forsaken South American banana republics for some tin-pot, bemedaled dictator, and all the rest of it. In 1935 Göring had telegraphed him personally and, as the new commander of the *Luftwaffe*, had offered him a major's commission and one of the first German dive-bomber squadrons. He had jumped at the chance. He had been down to his last peso, living like a bum, racked periodically by fever, not even enough money to pay for a litre of gasoline to get his beat-up old Curtis into the air and flee the miserable banana republic in which he had found himself. It had seemed the end of the road and twice in the middle of the night he had been tempted to use his old service revolver and make a finish to the whole damned mess. Göring, his old commander, had saved him from all that. One year later there had been the Condor Legion, Spain and Conchita... Abruptly Göring straightened up, a new animation in his pale blue eyes. Suddenly he seemed a decade younger, his face skinnier, his shoulders erect in the plain white uniform, decorated solely by the *Pour Le Merité* at his neck, instead of the usual mass of medals he wore. He reached out a fat hand and, picking up the heavy silver flask on the desk in front of him, tossed it to Greim. 'Take a snort of that, Walter,' he said, his voice level and confident. 'It's best Frog cognac. You look as if you could do with it.'

Greim clicked his heels and began, '*Herzlichen Dank, Herr Reichsmarschall* —'Cut out the crap, Walter!' Göring interrupted the formality in the crude manner of the old days back in the mess. 'I'm Hermann to you. Relax. Hell, man, in those times, we used to go horse-stealing together! Now put a slug of that frog firewater behind yer collar.' He grinned hugely.

Outside they had found the body. Hastily Greim put the flask to his mouth and took a deep drink. Hermann was right. It was top-class stuff unlike the German *kognak* they served in the mess. He gasped and wiped his mouth with the back of his hand. 'Well,' he said emboldened by Göring's previous statement, 'where's the fire, Hermann?'

Abruptly he grinned. It was exactly the same question he had asked the man opposite him in 1937 when he had been hurriedly summoned to the Air Ministry in Berlin and been told by Göring that 'volunteers' were required urgently for Spain. The Führer had decided to help the hard-pressed Franco and form the 'volunteer' Condor Legions to fly for the Spaniards. He had 'volunteered' immediately.

'Everywhere, but in your particular case, France. To be specific, the Meuse.' He waited, weighing up Greim's hard face with the nasty four centimetre scar to the left of the mouth, the cynical lips, but the sad eyes.

Greim grinned. 'Don't play games with me, Hermann,' he said slowly, taking another slug at the French cognac. 'I'm not from yesterday. You've got an assignment for the Black Knights. Spit it out.'

Göring wagged a fat finger at him, adorned by three gem-heavy rings, 'What a way to talk to the Führer's successor. Have you absolutely no respect?'

Greim shook his head slowly. 'Flogged it all to a Chinese pawnbroker back in Kansas City in '31. It went the same way as my medals.' Outside the firemen were dragging out an inchoate black and crimson mess, to which scraps of charred uniform still adhered. The parachute and harness straps had been burnt away by the searing heat, but underneath that charred crust, Greim could imagine the still white-hot buckles which had gnawed their way through to the very bone. 'The late Ensign von Dorn,' he said, as the rest of the Black Knights, dressed in black leather jackets now with white silk scarves at their throats, snapped to attention and saluted their comrade.

Göring nodded, as if it were not very important. 'The shitting SS,' he commented, as if that were explanation enough. 'Now back to the Meuse. Have you heard of a General … er Erwin Rommel?'

Greim shook his head.

'Frankly I hadn't either. But apparently he, too, is one of these March violets who have the Führer's ear these days.' The bitterness in Göring's voice was clearly evident and Greim realized again that his old wartime commander was afraid that he was on the way out; that there were too many newcomers enjoying Hitler's favour these days.

'He was on Hitler's staff as a colonel in the campaign in Poland and now the Führer has given him a panzer division and promoted him to general. He is, in other words, an up-and-coming man and as you know, my friend, the former chicken farmer has an eye for up-and-coming young officers.'

'You mean Himmler?'

'Yes, that damned chicken-farmer and his damned SS! So what does he do? I shall tell you, Walter, my old friend. Himmler approaches the Führer and has the audacity to *offer* your squadron as this Rommel's flying artillery! I mean the nerve of it! *I* am the head of the *Luftwaffe*, including the First SS Stuka Squadron. *I* do the offering. *I* make the decisions as far as the *Luftwaffe* is concerned. Oh, for God's sake, Walter, pass me that damned flatman. I need a stiff one!'

Obediently Greim handed him the ornate silver flask. Göring uncorked it and took a great swallow, his jowls wobbling as he drank greedily. 'They're not really ready, you know, Hermann,' Greim said, as Göring wiped a pudgy hand across his lips, then as an afterthought brought out a pure silk handkerchief reeking of perfume and dabbed them with it. 'My Black Knights are too arrogant, too headstrong, too full of a desire to die. I haven't broken their spirit sufficiently yet. They haven't learnt that a good soldier is he who doesn't die himself, but he who makes the enemy die.'

Göring shrugged carelessly. 'Frankly I couldn't care less about your Black Knights. They are SS and that suffices for me. But what I *do* care about,' Göring poked his fat chest with his thumb angrily, 'is the reputation of the *Luftwaffe* to which you belong, Walter!' Greim looked at him puzzled. Outside they were shovelling what was left of young von Dorn into an asbestos body-bag. Automatically Greim noted how pale his bold Black Knights had turned and told himself, they'd learn, they'd learn. This was the way it would end for many of them before the war was over. 'I don't understand, Hermann.'

With a grunt, Göring rose and waddled over to the big map of North-West Europe which decorated one wall of Greim's office. 'You know the general picture. In a matter of days now we shall attack west against the British and French. The frontline squadrons and naturally the army units too are already in position behind the West Wall, the whole length of the frontier from Strasbourg to beyond Aachen. Naturally the Army chiefs will not risk a head-on assault against the French Maginot Line — here!' He traced the course of the massive French fortified line which ran the length of her eastern front with Germany and on to their frontier with Belgium. 'Instead they will outflank the Maginot by attacking through Belgium, Holland and Luxembourg.'

Greim nodded. He knew something of the plan. His own Black Knights were only a hundred kilometres from the Belgian frontier as the crow flies, transferred here a week ago as, he had thought up to now, a reserve squadron. At the headquarters of the Air Fleet, he had already been told that the whole of the *Wehrmacht* in the west was on red alert status and he had concluded that it would be only a matter of days now before the balloon went up. All winter, ever since Germany had defeated Poland in the autumn of 1939, there had been nothing but patrol activity on the Western Front. Back in the Reich they mocked the war as the '*sitzkrieg*'. Now the 'sitting war' would soon be over — and it seemed that the Black Knights were going to play a role in the fighting after all. He waited for Göring's

. explanation with a growing feeling of apprehension.

'Now this fellow Rommel has been given command of the Seventh Panzer Division — one of those light divisions which did very badly in Poland — and naturally he is out to make a go of it. His nominal task is to push through the Ardennes Forest, drive into Belgium and help his corps secure a crossing of the River Meuse near Dinant.'

Greim nodded and wondered what was coming.

'Naturally the French will react — we already know their contingency planning for any attempt to outflank their vaunted Maginot Line. They will march into Belgium and attempt to cut off our drive before it reaches Northern France. That is where your *Black Knights*,' he emphasized the name contemptuously, 'come in. Our glory hunter, this damned Swabian upstart Rommel, will see the French counter-attack as an ideal means of grabbing the headlines for himself and his division, 'Göring saw the look on Greim's face and said hastily, 'Oh, yes I'm right, Walter. All these young generals are like that these days. They're worse than shitting film stars. So what will he do? He'll order his division to march to the sound of the guns and attack — *and*,' Göring pointed a manicured forefinger at Greim's heart, as if it were a stiletto, 'your damned Black Knights will be leading that attack, acting as his flying artillery and winning the kudos of the subsequent victory *not* for the *Luftwaffe*! Oh no, not for us who pioneered the weapon in Spain,' Göring's eyes narrowed to angry slits, '*but for that goddamned chicken-farmer with his skinny knock-knees and four-eyes — HEINRICH HIMMLER!*' he spat out the name, as if it were that of his most deadly enemy, little bits of saliva dripping from his painted lips down to his powdered hairless chin. 'That's who will get the glory.'

If the situation had not been so serious, Walter Greim would have laughed out loud at the look on Göring's face. He was just as vain as the rest of the Party big shots. He didn't care a hoot about the *Luftwaffe*. What he cared about was his personal reputation just like the others. 'So what do you expect me to do, Hermann? I can't give orders to a full general, you know.'

'I know … I know,' Göring snapped irritably. 'Let General *shitting* Rommel do as he pleases! He does not concern me — or you. What I want you to do, Walter, is to restrain those arrogant young aristocrats of yours.'

'Restrain them?'

'Yes,' Göring barked. 'Ride them *hard*, very *hard*, as *hard* as you wish,' he emphasized the word by slapping his beringed hand on the table each time. 'You will have my fullest support and cover. I do not want your Black Knights undertaking any death-and-glory missions at that damned Rommel's request. They will take their orders exclusively from you, Walter, and you, in your turn, take your orders exclusively from the commander of the Second Air Fleet.' For a fleeting moment, Greim caught a glimpse of that old Major Göring of two or more decades before, chewing out some young pilot who had buzzed the field or not kept the light battle formation which was typical of the Richthofen Squadron, his eyes like ice, his thin-lipped mouth an angry slit. 'We of the *Luftwaffe* are in control of First SS Stuka Squadron and not Himmler or this Rommel. *Verstanden?*' he barked.

'*Verstanden!*' Greim snapped back, though he spoke with more confidence than he felt. His young SS aristocrats were going to be a tough bunch to control, especially under active service conditions.

'Any questions, Walter?' Göring asked, reaching for his gold-braided cap and his bejewelled marshal's staff which Greim judged would have been worth a small fortune in any pawnshop he had ever known in the States.

'Yes, Hermann. When?'

'Five thirty-five on the morning of tenth May, 1940,' Göring answered. Greim gasped. 'But that's in three days' time!'

'Exactly and if my memory serves me correctly your squadron will be moving up to a forward field at the Eifel township of Bitburg in forty-eight hours.'

'But Hermann, there is so much to be done,' Greim stuttered, 'I mean I visualized the squadron's role as that of a reserve unit... There's ammo to be packed, the crates to be serviced, spare motors...! A thousand and one things —'

With an imperious wave of his baton, Göring ordered him to stop speaking. 'Major Greim,' he said with undue formality, now every inch of his massive bulk exemplifying the fact that he was the Commander-in-Chief of the most powerful air force in the world. 'Quite frankly, I don't care a hoot if the Black Knights ever get into action and if they do, well, they are Germans I suppose, but I would not waste any tears if they did not come back. All that concerns me — and you — is that the First SS Stuka Squadron achieves no glory, *not* one single mention in the newspapers so that the chicken-farmer can gloat over it. For me and the general public the Black Knights do not exist. I wish to keep it that way, Major Greim.'

· With that he touched his baton to his gold-rimmed cap and departed, leaving Greim standing rigidly to attention staring stupidly at the map of France...

CHAPTER 3

'*SILENCE IN THE KNOCKING SHOP!*' Sergeant Hanneman's tremendous voice cut into the noise and the excited chatter of the sergeants' mess with the traditional call to order.

Obediently the other air-gunners and NCOs of the ground staff turned their beer-flushed, sweating faces towards the big tough Air Gunner with the broken nose and scar-pitted face, the result of a nasty little encounter with a Polish anti-aircraft gun outside Warsaw, the previous September.

'You know why we're here,' Hanneman cried, a fist like a small steam-shovel clutched around his beer mug, as if he expected that 'Slack Arse' Schmidt, his running mate who was sitting next to him, might steal a quick sup if he weren't very careful. 'We're off at dawn to the front, and we all know what that means?'

Next to him Slack Arse simpered in a drooling falsetto, 'But you'll still tuck me up in bed at nights won't you, dear Senior Sergeant!' The 'peasants', veterans to the man of the war in Spain and the campaign in Poland, laughed and grinned, and Hanneman said, 'If you're not careful, you perverted little banana sucker, I'll tuck my nine millimetre up your slack-arse — *sideways*!... Now let's get on with it before the great,' his brick-red face contorted into a sneer, 'honour of *their* presence is bestowed on our humble selves.'

Someone farted contemptuously and there was a great roar of approval.

'I appreciate the sentiment one hundred per cent,' Hanneman agreed. 'Indeed I should like to shit on the black bastards from a great height, but then there is the C.O. to consider. He can't help it if he's got a bunch of arrogant shits like that as his pilots.'

There was a murmur of agreement from the others. Major Greim spoke their language. He was one of them. He could outfly any one of them, outshoot even Slack Arse Schmidt, and at a pinch, he would roll up his sleeves and tackle some nasty little engine problem with the crew chiefs. They all liked their tough cynical C.O. with his greying hair and casual ways, who smoked the same cheap workingmen's cigars as they did and had been known to give some horny peasant a weekend pass to attend his 'grandmother's funeral' — without asking a single question.

'All right, so we've got to live with them. Naturally the black bastards think they are hot-shot pilots, the world's greatest gift to the German Air Force. By the Great Whore of Buxtehude,' Hanneman cried in exasperation, 'most of us were flying when that lot were still sucking titty! But as I said, we've got to live with them, even if it's only for the Major's sake — and, comrades, to save our own necks too.' He looked around their red, suddenly solemn faces craftily. 'Cos don't make any mistake about it, mates, that lot are glory hunters. You might think that that Viennese sweet-talker Furst Schwarz is easy-going or von Heiter, with his stupid jokes, is all right. But they're the same as that arse-with-ears Baron Karst or de la Mazière. They're out for adventure, brave deeds, tin and promotion,' Hanneman lowered his voice almost to a whisper — '*and death!*'

The big tough, scar-faced sergeant let his words sink in and even the incurable optimist Slack Arse Schmidt at his side looked glum, abruptly.

'Now it don't matter one dry fart whether or not *they* die, but it does matter whether *we* die, comrades.'

'But what can we do about it, Hanneman?' Papa Dierks, Hanneman's crew chief, a white-haired sergeant who was reputed to be so old that he had fought in the Battle of Waterloo, asked plaintively. 'What can we do about it, Papa?' Hanneman echoed with a snort, 'I'll tell yer. We'll watch the slack-assed shits. Any attempt to get us peasants involved in some kind of piggery in order to cover their heroic chests with tin — and we sabotage it. I don't know how, comrades, but we will.' He pulled down the corner of his right eye significantly. 'Soon we will be going into action. Now from here on in, the motto is *wooden eye be on your guard*! Agreed, comrades?'

'Agreed!' they roared back.

'Then what are we waiting for?' Hanneman yelled enthusiastically, raising his litre mug of beer. 'Let's sink some of this good suds before the arrogant shits honour us with their presence. Remember after tomorrow we'll be supping frog beer — and that's worse than a one-legged whore's piss. *Prost, Kameraden*!' Carried away by the sense of comradeship and the knowledge that on the morrow they'd be back at the front once again, a hundred hoarse voices echoed the cry enthusiastically. '*PROST*!'

A hundred metres away in the officers' mess, Major Walter Greim slumped in the battered leather armchair at the edge of the big, smoke-filled room, heard the wild cry and told himself, he'd better be getting his Black Knights over there and have their visit done with so that his noncoms and air-gunners could get on with the serious business of drinking; for this night as was tradition in the *Luftwaffe*, they would get 'as high as a howitzer', as the peasants called it. By morning there would be 'beer corpses' everywhere on the base and many air-gunners would be moaning and sucking at the oxygen cylinders to get some relief from their skull-splitting headaches, as if they were drinking mother's milk. Tonight they'd make a night of it, that they would, over there in the Sergeants' Mess.

Greim took a last suck of his old pipe and looked at the officers as they clustered around the old piano singing, thumping its long-suffering black top in tune to the song. '*Wir Fahren Gegen Eng-e-land*', faces flushed with drink and youthful excitement. It could have been a scene from any air force officers' mess that he had ever been in, with the battered chairs, the chamber pots lined up on the window sills from which they drank beer for a wager, the stolen sign from the deutsche *Reichsbahn* nailed up above the fireplace with its legend, 'It is not permitted to use the latrine when the train is stopped,' and everywhere, of course, models and pictures of aeroplanes — there was even a model of a Tommy Spitfire hanging from the ceiling of the 'piss corner' outside.

The pilots looked little different too. Young, handsome, elegant in their uniforms, but somehow careless in them — a button undone here, a pocket flap open there, they looked almost the same as *Luftwaffe* pilots. They had the same affectations, too. Hanno von Heiter ran to a tiger cub on a chain, which he had baptized 'Churchill'. Furst Schwarz, the scion of an impoverished Austrian noble family, kept a battered Horch tourer in which he raced away nights to make ever new contacts, returning the following morning with a pair of silk knickers flying from his aerial, if he had been successful. Even Baron Karst, the senior flight commander — dour, ambitious and a fanatical National Socialist — affected a riding crop, monocle and riding breeches in which he flew, as if they were back in the old days of Richthofen's Circus.

But although they got blind drunk like other pilots often did, chased skirts in most of their off-duty time, periodically wrecked the mess on 'sports' evenings, there was something different, he knew, about his Black Knights. All of them, sons of the old penniless German-Austrian 'high aristocracy', had joined the SS not only because they believed fervently in the 'New Order' propagated by the Führer, but also because it represented a means of getting back to the top for them. They knew their Himmler, who was born at the old Bavarian royal court where his father had been the tutor to the crown prince. The head of the SS idolized the aristocracy from the depth of his petit bourgeois heart. He would do anything for them, and they had seized the opportunity that he and his black guards had offered them. The First SS Stuka Squadron was their chance of regaining their old pre-1918 prestige and importance, and none of them would allow anybody or anything to stop them reaching that aim.

Greim paused in his observation of his men and the flight commanders, his gaze falling on Lieutenant Detlev de la Mazière, the most junior of his commanders. Tall, lean, bronzed still from the winter's skiing, his blond hair a little longer than regulations demanded, Detlev was the spirit and soul of the Black Knights, and seemingly as fanatical and as arrogant as the rest. Yet, Greim thought, the young aristocrat had a heart. He knew how to handle the peasants well enough — after all he came from a family of officers which had been accustomed to giving orders for two centuries or more — and having them obeyed. His commands were accompanied by the word 'please'. He was not scared of pitching in and helping to load ammunition belts or gas from the bowser. Occasionally, too, he'd stop and chat with the 'old heads' like Papa Dierks, the crew chief, offering them a cigarette from his solid gold cigarette-case and asking them about their humble homes and their families. Naturally, Greim told himself, an officer with his century-old Prussian background would be used to that sort of thing. It was something that the de la Mazières would have always done on their estate in that remote East Prussian backwater; yet somehow, Greim suspected, there was something genuine and natural in the manner in which the tall handsome young officer did it.

He put out his pipe and stepped to the middle of the smoke-filled mess. '*Meine Herren,*' he commanded.

Schwarz at the piano changed from the dour marching song into a quick snippet of Strauss, ending it with a quick flourish along the keyboard, beaming up at the Squadron Commander with his much too beautiful Viennese smile which had been the downfall of far too many romantically inclined German 'maidens' these last few months and said, 'Your Excellency, the floor is yours!'

Greim bowed gravely, 'Have a thousand thanks, Highness,' he mocked.

'Excellency,' Furst played the game and gave him another flourish of the keys.

Hanno von Heiter's tiger cub growled at the noise and the tall slender young officer, elegant in his black uniform with the silver runes gleaming at the collar, tugged at the chain and snapped, 'That's enough of that. Down Churchill!'

The officers laughed and Greim said, 'All right, gentlemen. First I should like to thank you all for your efforts of the last twenty-four hours. You have done an outstanding job of getting the squadron ready —' he paused significantly. The smiles, the grins vanished now, even 'Churchill' stopped growling, as if he, too, were waiting for the Major's next words. The men already knew, for he, Greim, had passed on the word to Hanneman, one of his veterans of the Condor Legion. Now it was the turn of his unbloodied officers to know their fate — 'for action,' he completed his sentence softly.

The uproar was instant. Men burst out laughing. Others slapped one another on the back. At the piano Furst thumped out a few bars of the *Horst Wesel Lied*. Karst, the fanatical Nazi, snapped to attention and faced the highly coloured picture of Adolf Hitler on the wall and cried in a fervent ringing voice, '*Heil Hitler!*' Only young de la Mazière bit his bottom lip, his blue eyes suddenly grave, as if he might well have found it wrong to show so much enthusiasm for a matter which could only end in blood and misery. Greim waited patiently, telling himself not to be cynical about the Black Knights' reaction. Hadn't he been the same in January 1918 when his whole class had volunteered for the front straight from the *Gymnasium* and had marched singing through the old cobbled streets to the recruiting depot? He and little
Klein, who had lost both legs as an infantryman in the last great German offensive of that March, were now the only two survivors of those eager seventeen-year-olds. 'Gentlemen,' he broke in finally, 'I have only two things to tell you at this moment. One is that when you go into action, everything *won't* go to plan. Things will go wrong. They always do. Prepare for that eventuality *now*.'

Baron Karst frowned, his face dour, as if to say that nothing the Führer planned could ever go wrong. The Lord God above simply wouldn't allow it.

'Two, look after those ground crews and air-gunners of yours. The first will ensure you keep flying, the second will see your back is covered, perhaps even save your life, when a Tommy Hurricane or a Frog Potez gets on your tail, which they will one of these days, believe you me. Therefore treat your men well.'

Baron Karst's frown deepened even more.

'Now gentlemen you will accompany me to the Sergeants' Mess. They are already waiting for you. There you will accept a drink. It has always been the custom in the *Luftwaffe* to do so on certain special occasions such as this. It ensures good comradeship and teamwork.'

'Must we go through with this petit bourgeois nonsense, sir?' Baron Karst snapped in his harsh East Prussian voice, a sneer on his dark, dour face. 'All that beer, that thick-headed NCO boredom, the bawling of songs.' He jerked his thumb in the direction of the Sergeants' Mess from which came the drunken strains of 'Oh, *Du Schoener Westerwald*', accompanied by the thumping of stone beer mugs on wooden tables.

'Yessir,' Schwarz at the piano pleaded, 'especially as this is going to be our last night. I don't want to waste it. I've got a really hot number lined up in Koblenz. They say she has to keep her panties in the icebox — she's that hot!'

'Watch you don't burn your fingers,' Hanno von Heiter cracked, as the protests rained in from all sides, while Greim stood there craggy-faced and silent, staring into nothing, or so it seemed, eyes without emotion. In reality his mind raged at the young arrogant swine, who in due course would use and abuse their noncoms to cure their throatache but weren't prepared to have anything to do with them socially.

Suddenly, however, help came for Major Greim from an unexpected quarter. De la Mazière swung round on his angry, red-faced comrades and held up his arms for silence. 'Listen, comrades, of course the Squadron Commander's right. We do need them — and they're not really bad chaps — *for the*

Luftwaffe!' He winked hugely and his sally was greeted by whistles, grins and cries of 'pfui'.

He turned on a waiting Greim again and said, 'Can't we compromise, sir?'

'Compromise?'

'Yessir,' de la Mazière said eagerly. 'One glass of suds, another glass of that cheap firewater they drink and then off we go on our various ways. After all, sir, it *is* our last night.'

At the piano Schwarz ran his well-manicured fingers over the keys and whipped out a few bars of '*A Wandering Vagabond Am I*'. Greim's craggy face relaxed into a cynical grin. 'You joined the wrong service, de la Mazière. You have the gift of the forked tongue. You should have joined von Ribbentrop.'

'Oh la, la,' Hanno von Heiter simpered, 'a forked tongue. Wouldn't that make him popular with the ladies!'

Baron Karst slapped his riding boot with the crop he affected, eye gleaming angrily behind his monocle. He hated any mention of sex; he felt it was a personal affront to the Führer, who everybody knew lived like a monk. 'Oh, come on,' he snapped in irritation. 'Let's get it over with. Let's visit those thickheads of the NCO Corps.'

As a body they trooped into the warm May night towards the sound of the singing, with Heiter's tiger cub tugging hard at his chain, making low angry growling sounds deep down in his throat, as if he couldn't wait to get over there and start champing up one of the peasants…

Everyone was drunk. Beer corpses lay scattered in the wreckage of the sergeants' mess on all sides. The air was blue with smoke. In the corner the pear-shaped wooden 'people's receiver' was thumping out brass band music in a deafening bellow. Empty beer and schnaps bottles rolled back and forth on the littered floor. A sergeant, naked save for his jackboots and helmet, staggered through the debris and shouting men with what appeared to be a fishtail stuck between his buttocks, crying drunkenly, 'Hey, get me, mates, I'm a shitting mermaid!'

The rest of his words were drowned by a tremendous burst of wind let off by a snoring NCO slumped over a beer-wet table in the corner that set the glasses on it rattling alarmingly. 'Gas alert — gas alert!' Sergeant Hanneman cried, eyes crossed, as if he were in extreme agony.

Next to him Slack Arse Schmidt dropped to the floor, clutching his throat and writhing back and forth, yelling, 'I'm choking … I'm choking!'

Hanneman grinned and reached for another litre bottle of beer. He gripped the metal cap with his teeth and ripping it off, poured another long satisfying draught down his throat. 'It's been a real fine beer-bust, Slack Arse,' he called above the racket to his running-mate on the floor. 'If they gave beer-busts like this every day, I wouldn't even mind serving with the bastards of the Black Knights!'

Those who were still capable of doing so, took up the cry, as if it were some kind of toast, swaying wildly as they raised their mugs, '*the bastards of the Black Knights…*'

In his quarters, Baron Karst frowned at the racket and told himself that Major Greim might well be an ace Stuka pilot, but he had no concept of handling men like that. All they understood was the knout. For centuries the Karsts had taught their serfs to fear them in that manner, not to love them. Love was for fools. He dismissed the drunken caterwauling swine of NCOs and took out his diary which he had sworn to himself he would keep now for the rest of the war. Carefully in that pedantic manner of his he underlined the date in red, '8th May, 1940', then picking up his fountain pen he wrote in his neat small hand, 'So now we have the great news. Tomorrow we go to the front!' Again he took up his red pen and underlined the words. 'One is expected to be afraid and nervous, I have read. Afraid I am not. I shall do my duty as a loyal son of my father and a true National Socialist. Nervous, yes, because I fear I might not have sufficient chance to serve Folk, Führer and Fatherland significantly. In the titanic struggle to come which will see the end of the lies and corruption of the Old Europe, I wish to play a full part. I want to help to build, with our Führer Adolf Hitler, a new order, clean, lean and honest like our beloved Germany. *Sieg Heil … Sieg Heil … Sieg Heil*.'

He dropped his pen abruptly and felt a sudden warm glow of pride. He was going to war at last. Now the drunken cries and bawdy songs coming from the noncoms were forgotten. There was no dirtiness and corruption in the Black Knights. Here was only devoted dedication to the New Order. They were the symbol of the New Germany, unburdened by the dirty, shabby compromises of the past. They were the young men who would run the Reich when the war was won.

On impulse he snatched up his red pen and wrote boldly at the foot of his entry for this day: 'BY THE END OF THE YEAR I SHALL BE A MAJOR.'

Next door, separated from Karst by a thin wooden partition, de la Mazière lay stretched out on his bunk, fully clothed, save for his boots, hands clasped beneath his head, smoking silently, watching the blue fumes ascend slowly to the ceiling. He had declined Hanno von Heiter's invitation to drive into Koblenz. 'We'll hardly need to stroll along the bank of the Rhine for more than five minutes, old horse,' he had urged enthusiastically, 'when there'll be a whole gang of them, juicy plump little Rhine pigeons, just pleading with us to allow them to have a little mattress polka in their bedrooms, especially me, with my Churchill here. I am particularly irresistible. The female pigeons simply can't keep their delightful little hands off me.'

De la Mazière had declined the offer and the Squadron's comedian had gone off with Schwarz in search of 'plump Rhine pigeons'. Somehow it did not seem right to spend their last night chasing skirt; somehow it seemed unworthy of their cause and the brave young men who had already died for it. Besides he wanted time to think, for in the days to come, he knew instinctively he would not have any.

He thought of his father, General de la Mazière, old impoverished and alone. This night he might well be sitting alone in that dark sad house, gently declining into a ruin. The first war had ruined them. That day that the 'Reds', as his father had always called them, had marched up the drive and seized the lands that the de la Mazières had owned in Prussia ever since they had fled France in 1780, had almost broken his heart. It had been worse than in 1918 when his mutinous soldiers had ripped the officers' golden epaulettes from his shoulders. Adolf Hitler had come along too late to save his Father from the great depression which had overcome him in the twenties. Now undoubtedly he would be sitting in the saddle which had once borne him into action in 1914 at the head of his division, surrounded by the memories of the de la Mazière past — the flags, the trophies, the yellowing photos, the romantic battle paintings of the 19th century — silent and brooding about the lost honour of the de la Mazières while the old clock in the dark mouldering hall ticked away time with metallic inexorability.

De la Mazière lit another cigarette from the glowing stump in his mouth. Outside there was a slow crunch of boots on the gravel. He knew without even peeping out beneath the blackout curtains who it would be. Major Greim. He would be doing his rounds for the last time before he turned in. He smiled softly. The Major was like an old mother hen, the way he fussed about his Squadron.

He dismissed the C.O. as the footsteps died away into the night. Now even the drunken NCOs had had enough. Their singing had stopped. There was no sound now save the mournful whistle of some train on the Koblenz-Cologne line rushing through an empty station far away and the spectral whisper of the night breeze in the oaks.

Suddenly de la Mazière was overcome by a great sadness unusual to his nature. Why? he asked himself. Was it for his old broken Father so far away on his lonely rotting estate? Was it the eerie quality of the dying day, which could never be recalled? Was it the knowledge that soon his life would be irrevocably changed; for he was going to the front, to battle, and perhaps die as so many de la Mazières had done before him? He didn't know. Slowly, very slowly, the tall young man stretched out on the bunk drifted into sleep, his chest hardly stirring, his lean frame perfectly still. To a casual observer entering that tight hot room at that moment he might well have appeared dead...

CHAPTER 4

The field was like a furnace. The hot sun cut the eye like the blade of a sharp knife. Blue heat ripples rose in a steady stream above the parched yellow grass.

To the west there was the continuous, ominous thump-thump of the heavy guns and down below on the narrow winding white road that led by Bitburg Field towards the new front, column after column of sweat-lathered young men in field-grey, laden down with weapons and packs slogged their way through clouds of dust towards the battle. Behind them came the tanks, squat, sinister and black, their aerials whipping the burning air like silver whips. It seemed as if the whole of Germany was pouring westwards in a new great barbarian *Völkerwanderung.*

On the field itself there were blue-clad mechanics running back and forth with spares, sweating mightily over engines, loading bombs, slotting belt after belt of gleaming yellow machine gun bullets, working full out to meet Major Greim's deadline; for this day the Black Knights were going into action for the first time. General Rommel — over there to the west — was in trouble. That heavy barrage thumping away, flushing the burning sky a light pink, were the guns of his 7th Panzer Division. They had run into trouble and were stalled already. Rommel's mad dash for the Meuse, it seemed, had come to a very abrupt end.

If Major Greim's pilots were perhaps a little jittery at the prospect of their first action so soon, the craggy-faced Squadron Leader himself was perfectly calm, his voice fully under control, as he briefed his officers lying there in the parched grass. 'So you can see the situation,' he concluded his assessment of Rommel's position, 'the General has been stopped on the eastern bank of the River Our by strong Belgian anti-tank and artillery positions on the other side. Our job is quite simple. We are to supply the aerial artillery to knock those guns out so that Rommel can start moving again … and I might remind you that time is precious. Every hour counts if the General is to reach his objective. Clear?'

'Clear,' they all echoed dutifully.

'*Großartig*. Now this is the drill. You may make notes.'

Obediently they began to scribble the essential points directly onto the skin on the backs of their hands.

'We stay at zero metres until we have crossed the German-Belgian frontier. I want the field-greys down there to be able to see us clearly. I don't want them shooting us up before we have got started. As soon as I give the signal we climb at full throttle to two thousand metres. The Our should be about five minutes away then. Incidentally absolute RT silence is essential.' He frowned at them warningly. 'I want no chatter among pilots because the Belgians will be listening and they do have British Hurricane fighters, remember. When I see the Our, I shall signal and we will turn at ninety degrees to port and steer a course of zero forty-seven degrees for sixty seconds exactly. That will bring us directly over the river between our own positions and those of Rommel — his men up there have been warned that we are coming. All the same, it is better to be careful. It wouldn't be the first time that some excited stubble-hopper has fired on his own planes. Now when…'

Fact after fact, Greim hammered home the details of their first mission, clearly, logically without emotion, while they scribbled furiously to take them all down. He spoke as if he prepared missions like this every day that dawned, while their hearts beat like trip-hammers and their minds raced furiously at the thought of what was soon to come.

'Now you rear-gunners, one final piece of advice to you,' he turned to the veteran NCOs. 'Once we are over the target and we can break RT silence, I want brief and absolute clear indication of any enemy by the clock code speaking slow and quite distinctly, got it? You know the sort of thing — enemy at six o'clock … enemy at ten o'clock? You are flying with combat-inexperienced pilots. You must do your best for them and each number two covers his number one. Understood?'

'Understood,' they answered in a proud murmur. The C.O.'s little speech to them was quite unnecessary, they knew that well enough. They had flown half a hundred bombing missions in Spain and Poland; they knew exactly what to do. But the address had been for the benefit of the Black Knights, to show them just how important the peasants were; that they were not just unimportant passengers, but vital crew members. Greim dropped his pointer. 'Well, gentlemen, that's about it.' He looked down at his big Air Force chronometer. 'Let us syn —'

'— Circumcise our watches,' Hanneman beat him to it with the old joke. They laughed and the tension was broken.

Major Greim gazed at their young excited flushed faces as if he were seeing them for the very first time, trying to imprint their features on his mind's eye for all time, just in case… 'All that remains for me to do, comrades,' he said, his voice suddenly warm and emotional now, all cynicism fled, 'is to wish you all good hunting — and good luck!'

Next minute they were all running heavily, burdened as they were in their heavy leather flying gear, for the waiting planes.

Now a deep silence hung over Bitburg field. All eyes were fixed on Major Greim standing upright in the cockpit of his fighter, eyes fixed on his watch. By each aircraft the ground crews tensed, sweat pouring down their faces, fingers poised on the switch of the auxiliary starter batteries.

Further beyond others stood ready with their fire extinguishers. The heat and tension were almost tangible.

Twelve hundred hours. Greim glanced around his waiting pilots. He started to manipulate his pumps. There was a deep whine, a rasping groan. Slowly, very slowly, his propellers began to turn. Behind him his flight commanders switched on. This was it.

De la Mazière called, 'All clear — switches on!'

He fired his motor. The Jumo caught first shot. With a deafening roar, the 1,200 HP engine burst into life. All around him engine after engine caught. Frantically the mechanics, bodies glazed in sweat, dragged away chocs and starter motors. The gull-winged planes quivered frantically like highly strung horses at the starter's gate, impatient to be off.

Slowly they started to roll forward to line up behind their flight commander, their black wings glinting in the sun, all eyes on the little control tower now.

Bathed in sweat, nerves tingling electrically, de la Mazière pulled down his goggles. Behind him *Feldwebel* Schmidt took one last furtive slug from his flatman of neat gin and said a quick prayer, though he had not been in church these twenty years or more.

Twelve hundred and ten. De la Mazière gasped audibly. A white flare sailed in a glowing arc from the control tower. It was the signal. Fascinated he watched as the signal rocket hissed to the parched field like a fallen angel. To their front

Greim raised a gloved hand, opening his throttle with the other.

Eyes glued to Greim's tail, hands wet and slippery with sweat, de la Mazière did the same. They all did. Slowly, awkwardly, they started to bounce across the rough field. Greim's tail went up. The Stukas' did as well. They were nearly off. A ragged faint cheer came from the ground crews. De la Mazière felt his mouth was strangely dry. There was a disordered thumping of his heart right down to his stomach. His temples were clammy. He caught a last glimpse of Churchill, broken free from the mechanic detailed to hold him, running crazily after the planes, chain trailing behind the tiger cub, and then they were airborne and the field was falling beneath them at a tremendous rate…

They flashed over the frontier, a solid mass of black, packing as much punch as a whole corps of artillery. Below the little hill roads winding through the thick firs of the Ardennes were packed with marching columns and endless convoys of trucks and tanks. A dive-bomber pilot's dream, Major Greim thought grimly, as the white faces flashed up to look at them everywhere, and here and there a field-grey waved bravely. On they went. Now to his front Greim could see the hazy black clouds which indicated the shelling and the front, interspersed by thick spurts of cherry-red flame as yet another shell exploded. Now the countryside below was becoming emptier and Greim told himself that now they were really getting close to the front; the line was always an empty place. They roared over a group of tanks, their long cannon drooping, their tracks scattered behind them like broken limbs, a little hillock of fresh brown earth in which their crews had been hurriedly buried, to one side. All of them bore the silver and black cross of the

German Army. Greim bit his lip. He could see that this new General — Rommel — was taking some stick. The Belgians were fighting back more fiercely than the High Command had expected. He started to climb.

One minute later he saw the silver snake of the Our crawling along a deeply wooded steep valley. He waggled his wings and was about to turn the squadron to port when he saw them. Two Hurricanes and he didn't need the roundels painted on their camouflaged fuselages to tell him that they were Belgian. If they caught his Black Knights preparing to dive-bomb, there would be a slaughter. He broke radio silence immediately. 'Hurricanes ... eleven o'clock,' he snorted. 'Eyes peeled you air-gunners ... *attacking!*' He felt his stomach contract, but he wasn't really afraid. The old thrill of the chase was too overpowering. Whooping, he broke to the right and roared towards the two Belgians. Climbing steeply, the Messerschmitt going all out, he did a half roll. The manoeuvre outfoxed the Hurricanes. Before they could complete their 180 degree turn, there they were. A slight pressure on the rudder. The first enemy loomed large and clear in his sights. It was too good to be true. At less than 200 metres away, all he needed was a slight deflection. It was as easy as falling off a log. He squeezed the firing button. The plane shuddered. His nostrils were assailed by the acrid stench of explosive. The leading Hurricane trembled violently. It caught alight at once. Tongues of greedy flame started to lick the length of its camouflaged frame. Smoke, black, thick and oily, began to pour from it. Desperately the Belgian, obviously inexperienced, flung his plane into a turn. A thick white stream followed it as it raced through the bright blue sky. Abruptly, with startling suddenness it exploded like a hand grenade. An eye-searing flash. A thick cloud of black smoke. Debris flew through the air. He broke to the right hurriedly to avoid it. Behind him the engine dropped in a ball of fire, followed by one of the Hurricane's wings, fluttering down like a whirling metallic leaf. There was no white blossoming of an opening chute. The unknown Belgian pilot had died with his plane.

Over the RT there came the excited congratulations of his pilots and Baron Karst's almost hysterical cry of '*Sieg Heil … Sieg Heil…*'

But Greim had no time for their congratulations. The other Hurricane was on to him now. A stream of lethal white tracer just missed him as he flung his plane into a tight turn. The Hurricane was slower than his Messerschmitt but could manoeuvre better. He dare not give the Belgian a chance to get on his tail, or he would never shake the devil off.

Now the tracer bullets were exploding all round him in a frightening deadly fireworks display. He flung his plane round desperately, his head dizzy, his arms aching already, and gasping for breath. Manoeuvring at this speed made the controls stiff and it was sheer hard physical labour to keep it up. Now he could feel the hammering of his temples and the sudden tic of his left cheek under the confines of the flying helmet. Still the damned Belgie kept after him.

He swung to the right desperately. The Belgian failed to outguess him. He raced on. Greim didn't give him a second chance. 'I'm too shitting old to play the gentleman!' he rasped to himself and breaking again in a crazy manoeuvre that wasn't in the text-book, dived after the Hurricane.

Suddenly there it was, filling the whole of the sights, every detail down to its squadron number blindingly clear. Greim swallowed hard. For an instant he caught a white glimpse of the pilot's startled face as he craned his neck to look backwards at him. Then he hesitated no longer. He pressed the firing button.

The first burst ripped the length of the Hurricane's fuselage. He could easily see the white eruptions of the explosive bullets as they ran along the length of the metal. His second shattered the pilot's canopy into a glittering spider's web. The pilot's head disappeared, and abruptly the shattered perspex was flushed a horrifying crimson as the Belgian's blood jetted wildly from his severed skull.

Carried away by the terrible thrill, the wild excitement, of combat, Major Greim almost forgot he was still heading for the stricken Hurricane. At the very last moment when a crash was imminent, he thrust his stick forward. His head slammed against the windshield. The dying Hurricane flashed by only metres away. One moment later the Hurricane exploded in a wild ball of scarlet flame, flaming debris falling to the war-torn countryside below like red rain.

'All right, boys,' Greim called in an exhausted voice, as the black and white identification panels of Rommel's vehicles stalled on the Our came into view, together with the white canvas arrows stretched out on the eastern bank pointing to where the Belgians were dug in on the other side. He did a victory roll out of habit and because it was expected of him, though he felt no sense of elation, triumph, just utter weariness and sudden depression, 'attack … *NOW!*'

CHAPTER 5

'Did you see *that*, Schmidt!' de la Mazière gasped, as the Major roared high into the sky to take up his protective position above the Stukas now racking up for the attack, 'I didn't know the Old Man had it in him!'

Slack Arse Schmidt swinging round his guns ready to ward off any attack grinned into his helmet. 'The Belgies'll have to get up a lot earlier if they want to catch the C.O. out, sir. He's a good 'un. He was doing that kind of thing when we was a twinkle in our old man's eye.'

'I expect so,' de la Mazière said and dismissed the matter as, in front, Karst's flight hovered in the blinding blue sky like black sinister hawks. In a minute, he knew, they'd dive.

Karst waggled his wings. Suddenly they were dropping one after another. With their sirens howling hideously, they fell at an impossible angle, hurtling downwards at a tremendous speed, as if nothing now could stop them plunging straight into the ground below.

Almost at once the Belgian flak opened up. Red and white tracer started to curve upwards, slow at first, but gathering speed by the second. Everywhere there was the flash of anti-aircraft guns. Brown and grey puffballs of smoke peppered the sky. De la Mazière gasped involuntarily. Karst's plane staggered violently. For an instant it disappeared into the smoke. Had it been hit? *No*, next moment he gave a sigh of relief. Karst was still hurtling downwards at that crazy speed. The Stuka vibrated violently. A myriad deadly black eggs tumbled from its blue belly. De la Mazière could visualize Karst's eyes popping from his head with the strain, face purple, pulling mightily at the stick, trying to drag the Stuka from the dive before it was too late. Then the Stuka was sailing upwards and down below there was a tremendous rippling effect, followed by puffs of dark brown smoke, split by lightning-flashes of purple flame, as Karst's bombs exploded the whole length of the river bank. 'Hot damn,' de la Mazière cried in excited admiration, 'right on the nose — every one of those pills!'

Now Stuka after Stuka fell out of the sky from the rack, hurtling through the cotton balls of flame and smoke, missing death and destruction by mere metres as the Belgians filled the sky with flak and tracer. Red and white tracer criss-crossed the burning heavens. Clusters of vicious-glowing luminous balls curved upwards on all sides. Venomous black puffs splattered the blue, while below the earth was churned up a light whirling brown time and time again as yet another bomb exploded, hurtling bits and pieces of men high into the air so it seemed to rain arms and legs.

'To all,' de la Mazière snapped into his throat mike, '*NOW*!'

He took one last deep breath. '*Here we go, Schmidt*!' he yelled.

'*Hals und Beinbruch*!', 'the gunner cried back.

De la Mazière thrust the stick forward and then he, too, was falling out of the burning sky into that crazy inferno below. In a flash his A.S.I. was flickering wildly at 400 kilometres an hour. He was falling in an almost perpendicular dive. The green needle of his altimeter flashed through the heights. *Two thousand metres ... one thousand five hundred ... one thousand.* He continued to hurtle downwards. At his temples the blood pounded away. He gasped for breath. Tracer streaked by on both sides of him in mad, lethal rain. The plane shuddered violently. Flak was being directed onto him. He heard the clatter of the shrapnel on the wings. Still he roared down.

Five hundred metres.

He caught a glimpse of a 37 mm anti-aircraft gun's barrel poking out of a haystack, a handful of madly running figures in strange uniforms, huge brown holes looking like the work of gigantic moles everywhere and then he knew he was low enough. He pressed the bomb release. The Stuka jumped. He had no time for the falling bombs now. He had to pull the plane from its dive before it was too late. He hit the rudder bar and jerked the stick back with all his strength. As usual his eyes were immediately veiled red with blood. The air seemed to be snatched from his lungs by an invisible hand. For an instant he blacked out, pinned to the back of his seat by the force of gravity. Then he was there again, gasping for breath like an ancient asthmatic.

'Right on target!' Schmidt roared enthusiastically. 'Kicked the Belgies right up the arse — '

He broke off suddenly. The Stuka gave a tremendous shudder. The stick was nearly ripped from de la Mazière's sweat-drenched hand. He started to fall immediately. Desperately he fought to conquer the Stuka's drop. Not daring to take his eyes off the ground and his controls, he cried, 'What is it, Schmidt?… What in three devils' name has happened?'

'We came too low … I think we were hit by our own eggs… There are two … no, three holes in the port wing … one of the landing flaps seems to be gone!'

'*Scheiße, verdammte Scheiße!*' de la Mazière cursed, his face crimson as he fought the Stuka, coaxed, pleaded with the plane to come out of the dive and then abruptly he was skimming over the ground at less than twenty metres, blinded by the showers of tracer that converged on him from all sides, criss-crossing, making him feel that the slugs were going to hit him straight between the eyes before curving off to one side at the very last moment.

He crouched, drenched in sweat, his heart beating like a crazy trip hammer. Instinctively he moved his head from left to right, as if to avoid the flying tracer. Desperately he hurled the stricken machine from side to side. Behind him Schmidt pounded away with his machinegun, swinging it from left to right, scything the ground with bullets, cursing furiously as he did so.

A flak position leapt into view, only metres away. Desperately de la Mazière kicked hard at the rudder to make the crippled plane skid and put them off their aim. Thank God! The Stuka responded. The stream of 20 cm shells flashed by to port — purposelessly. Almost too late he saw an obstacle. A line of trees along the Our. He banked instinctively. He hit full rudder. Again the Stuka answered. But not quick enough. There was a tremendous rending crash. De la Mazière hung onto the stick with all his strength.

'*Great crap on the Christmas tree!*' Schmidt firing away behind him gasped. 'Now the clock's really in the bucket!'

But it wasn't — this time.

The Stuka struck one of the trees, but its momentum kept it flying. The Belgians below who had come running out of their slit trenches expecting to find the Stuka crashed there, bolted back for safety, with Schmidt stitching the dust behind their flying heels with slug after slug. Men went down, bowled over mercilessly by that tremendous hail of fire, piling up immediately into a bleeding, screaming heap of twitching bodies.

Dazed by shock, his mouth parched like old dry leather, de la Mazière flew on instinctively. Fear twisted his guts horribly. His throat was full of bitter burning gall. His muscles seemed to have vanished. He could hardly feel his feet. He avoided a cable by metres. To his right another gun started to spit flame at him — and another. The Stuka was losing speed all the time. He was a sitting duck. Flame spurted from flak guns all along the Belgian side of the river from the dark-green firs which marched up the hillsides like spike-helmeted Prussian Guardsmen. He was not going to make it. It was impossible. At this speed he hadn't a chance. This was going to be his first and last mission. The last of the de la Mazières was fated to die without ever being able to restore the family's honour and fortune. It was the end!

'Hello, young hero,' a familiar cynical voice crackled to life in his earphones. 'Don't lose your head now … and tell that rogue behind you to stop using his peashooter … we're coming in — *NOW!*'

De la Mazière almost lost his grip of the stick. He did not even hear the thump-thump of the burst of tracer running the length of his fuselage. It was Greim and the Black Knights… *They were coming to save him after all! The Black Knights were on their way…* Two minutes later he was limping along surrounded by his comrades, their gunners blasting away to left and right, with Major Greim riding confidently at their head like a Mother Hen guiding her wayward chicks back to the roost…

CHAPTER 6

Now the storm coming from the East spread the length of the border, bringing with it fire and blood. Hordes of refugees flooded the road. Everywhere there were their carts, the barrows, the ancient buggies, anything with wheels, piled high with the pathetic bits and pieces of the fleeing peasants and topped always with a mattress — a miserable form of protection against the death which came hurtling down from the skies. They blocked the highways and the tracks. Surging east from Northern France, the *poilus* were stalled time and time again by the fleeing terrified civilians with their inevitable cry from the heart, '*les Allemands … Les allemands sont la!*' And already, creeping in through the cracks in the valleys, rumbling down the 'insurmountable' Ardennes hills, infiltrating along the village tracks of that remote country came the panzers, squat, black and sinister, leaving behind them the stench of diesel and yet another half-dozen dead Belgian soldiers sprawled in the ditches near their shattered smoking cannon like bundles of abandoned rags. Like fire-belching, primeval monsters they were everywhere, twitching their long overhanging cannon like the snouts of greedy predators, hungrily seeking a way out of the hills down into the lush green plain below.

Above were their comrades, covering the blue spring sky with the white criss-cross of condensation trails, racing across the hill-sides, dragging their evil black shadows behind them, searching … searching … always searching. And in the ditches the unshaven, scared soldiers would shake their fists at the burning sky and cry, '*Stukas … Stuka swine!*'

There was no escaping this German wonder weapon, this flying artillery, which could be summoned by the most junior panzer commander within minutes, as soon as he ran into opposition. They tumbled out of the sky like a mad avalanche. First they would be simply a rash of black dots on the blue horizon. A distant roar. But even before the alarm whistles had begun to shrill their dread warning, and the soldiers had started to pelt to the safety of the fields, they would be spiralling down in that death-defying dive of theirs, sirens howling, motors racing in an ear-splitting roar. Yet again, the deadly little eggs would fill the air, cutting it with a shrill, terrifying whistle and then all hell would be let loose.

That sledgehammer blow after blow of the howling and booming down time after time brought terror to the hearts of the soldiers. All along that bloody frontier the slit trenches and holes of the defenders were filled with mortally wounded and the dead — and even the dead were not left in peace as the ground quaked and quivered all around them. As for the living, their nerves had gone under that furious unmerciful bombardment from the air. Now their harassed unshaven exhausted officers could see how the flesh around their blood-scummed lips trembled all the time and how their eyes, wide, wild and staring, continually filled with tears at that tremendous unbearable, overwhelming roar as if they might break down and begin sobbing at any moment. The faces of the young conscripts were pinched and drained of all blood so that they looked like those of old men, about to expire. '*Mon dieu*,' the officers sobbed, as yet another of the *sales Stukas* came winging in for the kill, 'will it never have an end to it?'

But the tremendous pounding went on, while the spring sun stubbornly refused to slide beyond the fir spiked horizon and grant them the blessing of darkness and no bombs. Overnight young men went grey and became old. Older men went mad. Some frothed at the mouth, screaming hysterically and running out into the open begging the evil black machines and their grinning pilots to kill them, put them out of their misery once and for all. And at night when the Stukas had finally departed, men whimpered like animals in their trenches, talking to themselves and weeping, while others who had not prayed these many years, pleaded fervently to a God of Mercy to grant them just one dawn without Stukas, just a few hours of peace.

But in this terrible May of 1940, the God of Mercy was not listening. As the blood-red ball of the sun rose over the hills of the Ardennes, flushing the valleys with the first crimson hue of a new day, there they would be — those sinister deadly black hawks coming in from the east again — and that dread cry would rise yet once again on all sides. '*STUKAS ... THE STUKAS ARE COMING...*'

That May, each new day started for the Black Knights at four in the morning. The beam of the sentry's torch would blind the sleeper and the weary voice would say, 'Time ... time to get up, sir.'

The sentry would tick the officer's name from the check-board list he held, and leaving the warmth of his blankets, the pilot would stagger, drunk with sleep and aching all over from the previous day's flying, to join the others. It was like a meeting of sleepwalkers. Every day now they were flying three and four sorties for Rommel's Division and sometimes spent up to ten hours on 'readiness'. As a consequence they fell into their bunks worn out at night and woke up still exhausted. Gulping down a cup of black coffee, too tired to be hungry, smoking a cigarette here and there, they would stumble out in the ugly white light of the false dawn. Eyes heavy and unseeing with fatigue, they would reach for their parachutes, check their flying helmets and trail wearily to the planes which dominated their lives totally, obsessively now, as if the metal monsters were the masters and they simply their willing slaves. The mechanics would already be at work, warming up the engines, swarming over the planes, checking equipment, feeding in new belts of machine-gun ammunition, attempting to patch up the damage of the previous day's flying, filling the fuel tanks, a thousand and one tasks carried out with hands that felt as thick as sausages and with eyes so weary and sore, that they seemed to have been rubbed with sand. More than once Hanneman would observe to his running-mate Slack Arse Schmidt, as they stood at the edge of the field watching the zombie-like movements of both crews and ground crews, sipping an ice-cold bottle of beer (for he and his comrade lived off beer these days), 'Christ, Slack Arse, we can't go on much longer like this! Five solid days of it now and I bet we haven't had more than four hours' sleep a day all the time. Mark my words, Slack Arse, we're getting too tired ... too careless. One of these fine days soon, the Black Knights are going to cop a real packet. One day those arrogant black bastards are gonna get the purple shaft right up their aristocratic arses.'

And invariably Slack Arse Schmidt would answer, depositing his bottle in the already half-empty crate, mournfully, 'Don't forget, arse with ears, if they get shafted, we do too. We don't shit through the ribs either, yer know!'

But Sergeant Hanneman never seemed to have an answer to that enigmatic statement.

Yet when it seemed that the Squadron would never make another dawn attack, there would be Major Greim, washed and shaven, as full of cynical energy as ever, barking out commands, making jokes, slapping shoulders, pretending to boot Hanno von Heiter's damned tiger cub, Churchill, forcing his will on pilots and ground crews, dominating them with his personality and putting new strength into them until finally the white flare would curve into the grey morning sky from the control tower and they would be rumbling forward to the attack yet once again.

Then surprisingly on the evening of May 15th, as they fell out of their Stukas, their legs like rubber after ten hours' flying and combat, with only strength enough to plunge their haggard, begrimed faces into the waiting pails of cold water, they were received by the news that they were to be stood down. On the next day there would be no further operations. They were to rest for the next twenty-four hours.

Even Baron Karst, implacable and fanatical as he was, always eager for glory, heaved a scarcely concealed sigh of relief and sat down suddenly in the parched grass. Next to him Furst Schwarz said gratefully, 'Jesus Maria Joseph, thank God! If this had kept up any longer I know my outside plumbing would have seized up from excessive expenditure of energy ... which would be a sad loss to the female population of this world under the age of thirty.' Hanno von Heiter had chuckled and tumbled his little pet into the grass. 'It's in your honour you know — the Tommies have just gone and made that drunken old sot their new prime minister. Churchill is now to preside over the downfall of the British Empire!'

Only de la Mazière seemed unable to share the happiness and relief of the others as they lay there in the parched grass watching the evening fog come rolling in from the Eifel hills. There seemed no reason why the Black Knights should be stood down. Rommel's Division had now reached the left bank of the first great natural barrier stopping his dash to the great northern plain of France, the River Meuse. Surely he would need all the flying artillery he could get to cover his attack across it? His high brow creased in a puzzled frown. There was something in the air. He knew it instinctively. But what?

Major Greim was equally puzzled when he received the telephone call that night. For once his young pilots had eaten a real dinner though their mood had been subdued. They ate the dinner in silence and only the Austrian Furst Schwarz and Hanno von Heiter remained in the mess to drink a beer or two together. Greim had been about to join them, for he knew the mood in the mess bar was always a gauge of a squadron's morale, when the orderly had appeared with the message that he was wanted urgently on the telephone.

It was Rommel's aide, a pompous young man with an affected, overexaggerated Prussian accent who had attached himself to Rommel's rising star in the knowledge that it meant promotion for him in due course. 'Major Greim,' he barked as if he were on the parade ground at Berlin-Spandau in the days of the Old Monarchy.

'Yes.'

'You are alone, Major?' the aide rasped nasally.

'No,' Greim answered angrily, 'I'm lying in bed with two fat juicy whores who are transparently French spies! Of course, I'm damned well alone! What is it?'

The angry outburst had obviously taken the wind out of the cocky young officer's sails, for when he spoke again his voice was subdued and less confident. 'It is the General, sir,' he said. 'He has requested you come up here to St Vith for a briefing at six hundred hours tomorrow. The General will brief you personally.'

'Six o'clock tomorrow morning … a personal briefing?' Greim echoed in bewilderment. 'What is this? Is there something gone wrong?'

At the other end there was silence, but Greim could almost feel the young aide's mind racing, as he debated what he should now tell his listener. Finally he spoke. 'It's absolutely top-secret, sir,' he said carefully. 'But there have been — er — developments, sir.'

'What kind of developments, man?'

'I'm afraid I can't tell you that, sir, but the General is very insistent that you come here. We have arranged a provisional landing strip just outside the town... And, I know from the General that the Führer is informed of what has happened,' the aide added, already wise to the ways of senior officers with their constant attempts to obtain personal publicity and shine in the eyes of the Leader, for that was the way to gain promotion.

'How nice for him!' Greim snorted. 'All right then, I'll be there, but forget the blackout and keep the strip's landing lights burning brightly.' He flung a glance out of the window. It was nearly dark now but the fog was clearly visible. It was rolling in in ever thicker clouds. 'I shall be there at your HQ in about an hour. You can put me up for the night. *Ende.*' Without waiting for the aide to reply, he slammed down the phone onto its cradle, a worried look on his craggy face. First the Squadron was stood down, then this. Greim rubbed his bony scarred chin. He was wise in the ways of generals at war. Something had gone wrong, he knew it instinctively, and the ambitious Swabian General wanted his Black Knights to put it right for him again. The Black Knights were in for trouble...

CHAPTER 7

'I know ... I know,' Greim said reassuringly, as Sergeant Hanneman trailed beside him, laden with his flying gear and parachute. 'Air-gunners deserve a rest, too. But you're the best the Squadron's got and I need you, so you'll just have to grin and bear it.' He pulled the flatman from his back pocket and tossed it to the grumbling NCO, as they broke through the fog towards the waiting Fieseler Storch. 'Put a slug of that beneath yer collar for a start. In an hour's time we'll be in St Vith and you can sleep the sleep of the just this night.'

'In an hour's time!' Hanneman moaned, 'Not in this pea-souper we won't.' All the same he unscrewed the little flat bottle and took a deep and satisfying slug of the cognac it contained. Greim grinned and swung himself inside the little courier machine which could take off and land in less than two hundred metres which made it ideal for landing on some provisional air strip or other; for he knew of old that Army engineers who built the things usually had little knowledge of the real requirements of a pilot trying to set down on a bumpy grass field. Hanneman squeezed in behind him and weary and irritable as he was, immediately set about checking out the single MG 15 machine-gun with which the monoplane was equipped. 'Thousand rounds of 7.92 mm a minute,' he said to himself half-aloud, 'not a bad little pop-gun at all.'

Greim grinned as he went through the customary preflight inspection. Old Hanneman's bark was worse than his bite. If any nasty Frog, Belgie or Tommy did get on his tail this night, Hanneman would see him off very smartish, though in this fog he thought the eventuality highly unlikely. Satisfied he barked,

'All right, Hanneman, now don't start sawing wood back there. Keep a weather eye peeled. The fog's getting worse by the minute.'

'What you officers would do without us NCOs God only knows. Some of them need to be told to come in out of the rain —'the rest of his words were cut off by the sudden roar of the engine. A minute later the little plane was airborne and rapidly disappearing into the fog. Behind on the field, the lights went out one by one, and the fog curled itself around the huts with their exhausted snoring occupants like a soft grey cat. Now the Black Knights had exactly thirty hours left before their first great mission commenced…

They flew at a steady 100 kilometres an hour. Above the green glowing instruments, the perspex of the canopy dripped with a myriad rivulets of water. Some had already been forced through the cracks by the air pressure and both Greim's kneecaps were already marked by dark damp stains. 'Suppose I'll get rheumatism of the knees one of these days — if I live that long,' he told himself a little cynically, his mind still pre-occupied by the strange telephone call and what it boded for the Black Knights.

Behind him Hanneman was singing to the tune of the popular Army marching song of 1940, *'Auntie Hedwig, Auntie Hedwig, your sewing machine it goes not… I've tried all night to oil it, but it won't sew as I like it…'*

Greim grinned. The big red-faced boozer was in good form, his initial irritation vanished. Obviously the flatman would be almost empty by now.

Greim started to come down lower. He had been flying for some fifty minutes now. Soon he should be over the chain of high hills which ringed the little Belgian frontier town of St

Vith to the east. With a bit of luck the fog might be thinner in the valley so that he could spot the provisional field. Cautiously he trimmed back the Storch's speed to sixty kilometres an hour, slightly above stalling. At that speed he might just be able to see any damned high tension cable — in time.

Abruptly the thick grey clouds seemed to vanish and the Storch found itself in a kind of green *allée*, the colouring of the fog walls on both sides coming from the massed firs down below. It was uncanny. It was as if they were flying down a gloomy cavern, lit by an eerie funereal unreal glow.

Greim bit his bottom lip and flashed a look to left and right. Nothing but the endless green gloom of the forest. God in heaven, where exactly was he? Behind him Hanneman had abruptly stopped singing, as if he had sensed somehow that his C.O. was worried.

Greim swallowed hard. He knew he daren't ask for a course by radio. After all, for all he knew, he might be flying over enemy territory, and there were still pockets of enemy artillery and troops left behind in the Ardennes everywhere, waiting for the infantry which were following the panzers to mop them up. Where in three devils' name was north? Suddenly he realized that they were lost.

'Do you think I could get out now, sir?' Hanneman said in a little boy's voice, obviously reading his C.O.'s thoughts. 'I think I feel my migraine coming on again. I'd better lie down immediately and have a cup of weak herbal tea.'

Greim laughed. Hanneman, the big rogue, was just the man he needed on a tricky rotten night like this, when one felt as if one were all alone in the world. 'I know exactly how you feel, you horned-ox,' he said, as they were submerged by the damp rolling fog once more so that even the tips of the wings were no longer visible. 'God only knows where we are now.'

'What about coming down and landing — say on a road, sir?' Hanneman suggested. 'You know these crates can land on a five-mark piece. If we could make out a road, I could find a road sign or something. We could use that for orientation…' His voice trailed away, as Greim shook his head.

'Not a hope in hell, Hanneman,' he answered. 'There are too many trees in this region and too few roads. Besides I can't see my hand in front of my nose at this particular moment. I could not risk a blind landing.'

'But we can't keep on flying for ever, sir,' Hanneman objected. 'We'll run out of juice sometime or other.'

'We've just got to take that chance and keep on flying till there's a break in this shitting fog and we can see something. With a bit of luck those field-greys have a nice red beacon going to guide us in,' he added a bit lamely.

'Yer, and if my Aunt Sophie had a moustache she'd be my Uncle Franz,' Hanneman said in disbelief.

They flew on, the green needle of the fuel tank sinking ever deeper towards 'E' for empty.

The minutes ticked by leadenly. There was no sound now, save that of the engine and their own heavy breathing. They seemed like men trapped by time, moving through the grey wastes as if doomed to travel thus for eternity. But all the while, Greim glancing at that wavering green needle knew that time was running out for them. He *had* to find a landing place soon!

On impulse he decided to bring the Storch up. Perhaps it would be better higher. It certainly couldn't be worse. He pulled back the stick and rubbed at the inside of the perspex which was quite steamed up. Suddenly his heart missed a beat.

Outlined quite clearly against the mountainous corridor of fog, abruptly tinged a hard silver by the moon which had appeared from nowhere, there were a dozen black spots lumbering along, followed by six or more smaller planes.

'*Holy strawsack!*' Hanneman gasped, recognizing the planes sailing majestically to their front immediately. 'British Blenheims!'

'Yes,' Greim said through gritted teeth, still too shaken by the sudden apparition to be able to do anything but stare pop-eyed like some drooling village idiot, 'and escorted by a flight of Morane-Bloch fighters. It is a combined British-French attack force.'

'But what the —'

Greim cut him off with a harsh '*Schnauze!*'

Two of the French fighters had spotted them. In the harsh silver light of the moon he could see them quite distinctly as they waggled their wings at one another in a signal. He flung the little monoplane to the left. Almost immediately the French broke off from the formation and hurtled towards the Storch, machine-guns chattering, light angry-blue lights rippling the length of their wings.

Desperately Hanneman swung his single machine-gun round to meet the challenge, hanging on grimly, as Major Greim dived for the cover of the fog. The major braked suddenly. A stream of red-glowing tracer cut the sky to his front. Now he broke out into a lather of sweat, his left leg suddenly nervous with an abrupt tremor. For the other plane was swinging in to port in an attempt to cut off his retreat. In a moment they would have had it. He felt the veins thumping at his wrists and under his knees. For an instant he was as if paralysed, prepared to accept the inevitable.

Suddenly he thought of Conchita and the boy Miguel. He could actually see them, although they were nearly two thousand kilometres away in that barren, sunbaked Spanish village of theirs, staring up at him from the glass of the canopy, eyes liquid with tears, hands clasped together as if imploring him to do something — *anything.*

The instinct of self-preservation returned in a flash. He felt utterly cool and in control of the situation. He smashed his foot down on the rudder bar. Swiftly he swung the stick right back. The Storch howled in protest. Every single rivet screamed under the strain. Slugs pattered the length of the fuselage. There was a rending sound of something breaking. Abruptly the cockpit was filled with the acrid stench of burnt explosive. Behind him, Hanneman yelled in triumph. His little machinegun chattered at a thousand rounds a minutes. Like a flight of angry red hornets his tracer shot towards the second Morane. Even in that bad light, Greim could see the lumps of metal being ripped from the French fighter. Completely unexpectedly the plane disintegrated in midair. The turbulence hit the little Storch as if it had just flown into a solid brick wall.

With all his strength, the sweat streaming down his forehead and threatening to blind him, Greim fought the machine as it bucked and swayed with incredible violence, knowing that the stick would be wrenched from his hands at any moment; and then it was over and he was winging straight into that lovely, beautiful, darling thick grey fog…

'Hanneman,' Major Greim said with heartfelt relief as the red line of fires began to flicker merrily below and the first green signal flares started to ascend into the fog in welcome, 'there'll be a piece of tin in this for you. Undoubtedly this is the first Storch ever to shoot down a first-line French fighter.'

'Do you think I could request a quick transfer to the Pay Corps instead, sir?' Hanneman said in a weak voice. 'The wet stuff is still trickling down my left trouser leg. I don't really think I'm cut out for this kind of thing.'

Greim gave a weary grin.

Two minutes later they were taxiing towards the winking flashlights signalling them in and almost before Major Greim could unclip the canopy, the aide (for he was sure that the excited young officer with the splendid lanyard had to be General Rommel's aide) was stuttering furiously, 'Oh, my God, thank Providence that you made it… Thank … thank God. Terrible things have happened since I spoke to you!'

For one awful moment, Greim thought the handsome young lieutenant, his face hollowed out to a death's head in the light of the blue-capped torches which surrounded them on all sides, might well break down and begin to cry, but he caught himself just in time. Grasping Major Greim by the arm, digging his fingers into the pilot's flesh until it hurt, he stammered, 'Let us hurry, please sir! The
General will see you at once… '

Like a prisoner being led away to the slaughter, Major Greim, his weariness vanished in a flash, knowing instinctively that he was heading for serious trouble, let himself be guided to the big blacked-out school which was the headquarters of General Erwin Rommel…

CHAPTER 8

There was a flap on, he could see and hear that. Rommel's headquarters located in that big echoing 19th century school on the outskirts of St Vith was experiencing a one hundred percent, gold-carat flap. Here the clock was very definitely in the bucket!

As he stood there in the hall waiting to see the General, he could hear the snarl of motorbikes as leather-coated, dust-covered dispatch-riders came from and went to the front. Behind the closed doors telephones jangled constantly bringing ever more alarming reports from the line. Pale-faced clerks ran the length of the hall, clutching sheaves of papers, while staff officers strode to and fro, their faces set and grim. 'Good God in Heaven,' someone kept moaning in a shocked voice somewhere to the left, 'we never expected this. *Oh, Good God in Heaven!*'

Stolidly Major Greim puffed at his cigarette, seemingly oblivious to the excitement, fear and tension all around him. Under the yellow light of the naked bulbs, his craggy, lined face revealed nothing. In fact, his mind was racing, trying to put together the events of the evening. First the urgent telephone call. Then the British bombers with their French fighter escort. The Western Allies were obviously striking back in some form or other. The vaunted General Rommel had been caught with his knickers down about his ankles. Either he had already been shafted or was about to be shafted. Greim gave a little secret smile. The thought gave him a certain amount of inner pleasure. He had never very much liked ambitious — or innocent — men; they invariably caused trouble. His smile vanished and he frowned.

Naturally this personal summons to Rommel himself meant that his Black Knights — and the peasants, too, naturally — were required for some big op; and big ops always meant casualties. His frown deepened. So far he had brought them through their first week of combat safely. But could he restrain his arrogant young officers if they were given some special operation to carry out? He knew them. They would throw caution to the wind to gain the glory, medals and promotion that they all sought so desperately.

'*Herr Major,*' the aide's Prussian voice cut into his reverie. 'The General will see you now.'

Formally he stood to one side at the big door, spreading out his hands as if to carry Greim in like 'some damned stage butler in a third-rate comedy', Greim thought to himself contemptuously as he strode by the lackey.

A group of senior officers were gathered at the far end of the big room, which still bore the primitive paintings that children had made on its walls, listening while the small sturdy figure in their centre dictated a message to a sweating bespectacled clerk in a confident little bark, his accent noticeably Swabian.

That would be the famed General Rommel, Greim told himself and studied him for a few moments. He was sturdy and compact, perhaps about fifty, and there was no mistaking the power and authority that emanated from his dark square face, with its cleft chin, a sure mark of ambition and aggression. Rommel was on his way upwards, there was no doubt about that, 'but not at the cost of the Black Knights' lives,' a hard little voice at the back of his brain warned him urgently.

He nodded his head as if in agreement and then stiffened to attention as the General dismissed the harassed sweating clerk who scuttled from the room like a timid rabbit and turned his attention to Greim.

For a long moment he stared at the dishevelled, weary *Luftwaffe* officer, still dressed in his flying clothes, looking him up and down like a sergeant-major examining some particularly sloppy recruit before he gave him the full benefit of his rage. Slowly Rommel started to smile and for an instant his dark eyes sparkled, 'So the gentlemen of the *Luftwaffe* also get their arses dragged through the shit at times, too, eh, Major Greim.' His accent was pure Swabian now. Greim returned the smile, but inside his head the little voice said, as if in warning, 'Watch him, Walter, he's setting you up. He wants something real bad.'

Rommel stretched out his hand, 'Welcome to the Seventh Panzer Division, Greim. You look as if you could do with a drink.' He sighed wearily and for the first time Greim noticed the dark circles of worry and weariness under his eyes, 'We all do, I think, gentlemen.'

There was a murmur of agreement and Rommel clicked his fingers. As if he had been waiting behind the door for this very moment, the aide came in immediately bearing a tray, glasses and a bottle. 'Local rot gut,' Rommel commented, as the aide began to pour hastily, spilling some in his anxiety to please, 'but it's wet and alcoholic.' He accept a glass and raised it as if in toast to the third button of his tunic, arm extended at a forty-five degree angle, as regulations prescribed. '*Prost!*' he barked and tossed it down in one gulp.

The officers did the same and then the aide was dismissed and General Rommel got down to business.

'Major Greim,' he barked, one hundred percent professional now, absolutely confident, 'for the last thirty-six hours I have

been fighting the French Cavalry Corps and have beaten them.' He said the words without boasting, but simply as a matter of fact. 'But the French *have* achieved the classic aim of the cavalry — shielding their own forces while they occupied their main defensive positions along the River Meuse. Good. We expected this and will cope with them in due course. By dawn tomorrow we expect to be in a position to start
the river crossing at three points.' He let the information sink in.

So that was it, Major Greim told himself. The Black Knights were going to be used as aerial artillery to support Rommel's river crossing. He relaxed a little. That wouldn't be so bad. Rommel would obviously attempt to catch the enemy off guard so they wouldn't have time to mass their flak. He felt a little happier.

'Naturally the enemy air forces have been attacking my own forward positions all day long. They know what is coming of course. It was to be expected. The High Command has promised a wing of fighters for the morrow to help protect my hard-pressed men. However,' he paused and automatically Greim noted the sudden tensing of his strong jaw muscles and how his staff officers seemed to be holding their breath. Suddenly he knew, with the clarity of a vision, that he had not been called here to lead the Black Knights' attack on the Belgian-French troops dug in on the other side of the River Meuse. There was something else, something very nasty and dangerous in store for his Squadron. The crunch was coming, he knew it instinctively. Major Greim tensed apprehensively.

'ATTACK … ATTACK…' the shrill cries of alarm broke into the sudden heavy silence. Outside whistles began to blast. Someone began to bang an alarm gong. There was the sudden thump-thump of flak guns and the high hysterical chatter of a

Spandau. The door was flung open. The young aide stood there, his chest heaving, his face ashen. 'Sir ... sir,' he gasped and it gave Greim pleasure, real pleasure, to see that the supercilious young bastard was scared shitless.

'What is it, man?' Rommel barked, annoyed.

'An air attack, sir! They're coming in in swarms ... hundreds of th —'The rest of his words were drowned by the snarl of aeroplane engines flying full out and the thin whistle of descending bombs. Next moment the whole room rocked as they slammed into the ground just metres away. The lights went out, abruptly. Glass splintered. Greim hit the deck, as the blast raced through the window, filling the room with lethal razor-sharp splinters. There was a howl in the darkness. Next to Greim, lying pressed to the heaving floor, something red and obscene rolled to a stop. It was the severed head of the arrogant young aide...

Down below the fields, bathed a bright silver in the light of the 'bombers' moon', were strewn with bodies and still-burning half-tracks and tanks. Flak fire erupted from the guns all around the HQ, a massive drum-roll that echoed and re-echoed in the hills surrounding St Vith, wreathing the HQ in smoke, which was cut by the dazzling parabolas of the rapid-firing 20 mm quadruple flak guns.

Again a flight of the French bombers — Breguet 693s, Greim recognized them instantly — came hurtling in with a deafening roar, oblivious to the brilliant chains of tracers which barred their way. 'Here they come, General!' Greim yelled above the racket, as the two of them crouched there on the school's roof, for Rommel had insisted he would view the attack in spite of the protests of his staff officers who had fled to the cellars. 'They're coming in for the attack again!'

The lead plane staggered. It had taken a hit. Its port engine was already beginning to burn. Still the pilot held formation as the attackers started to level out, their bomb bays already open. 'Hold on to your hat, sir!' Greim yelled in warning. 'This is it!' There was the shrill howl of falling bombs. Cannon boomed. Machine guns chattered frantically. The plane with the burning engine suddenly fell out of the sky. At two hundred kilometres an hour it hit the ground. In a great cloud of flying dust, making an awesome rending sound, as its belly was torn out, shredding metal as it hurtled towards the school, its pilot obviously fighting to control it before it was too late, it crashed straight into a group of armoured cars, bowling them over as if they were children's toys. Next moment the whole group disappeared in a tremendous burst of flame.

'*Mein Gott!*' Rommel breathed, 'so *this* is what it's like!' Next moment he ducked, as the bombs began to explode all around them, showering the two officers with tiles and bits of masonry from the other side of the roof, the blast lashing their faces like a soft wet fist, dragging the very breath from their lungs so that in an instant they were gasping for their very lives like stranded fish.

Now the last Breguet came howling in, its every feature clearly visible in the lurid flames springing up everywhere. Red, white and green tracer zipped beneath its belly. It staggered alarmingly, as if it had suddenly bumped into an invisible wall. Half its tail had gone in a ball of fire. Still the desperate pilot pressed home his attack, thick black smoke streaming from the stricken plane now. Machine-gun fire ripped the port wing to shreds. Fragments of aluminium fluttered downwards like metallic rain. Greim bit his bottom lip in admiration, half-wishing the enemy pilot to succeed. Miraculously he managed to avoid another burst of 20 mm flak, racing up towards him at a rate of 1,000 shells per minute. Then his bombs came racing down. They ducked together yet once again. A column of trucks lined up in a field two hundred metres away were suddenly galvanized into frenetic electric action, being tossed back and forth like children's playthings, rearing up on their back axles, as if they possessed life of their own, before disappearing in a sea of flame and fire. Next moment the stricken French dive-bomber slammed into the hillside behind the HQ. Greim closed his eyes. He wished the French pilot had made it.

Rommel breathed a sigh of relief and started to slap the dust from his uniform as the flak stopped firing at last and from below came the shouts and cries of soldiers emerging from their slit trenches and cellars to find a transformed landscape, with trucks and tanks burning everywhere, the flames turning night into day.

'So that is what it is like to be at the receiving end of a dive-bombing attack,' Rommel said, awe in his voice, no trace of anger there at the losses the French had inflicted on his vehicle park. 'Magnificent, just simply magnificent! How brilliant of the Führer to have created in the Stuka squadrons the most formidable dive-bombing force in the whole world. If a handful of French bombers can do this,' he extended his hands to embrace the stark lurid lunar landscape below, 'what work of destruction can be carried out by a thousand Stukas. Nothing, simply nothing, would be able to stop them. It is General Douhet's dream come true. Stukas and panzers, Major Greim, it is an unbeatable team!'

Major Greim's face showed no enthusiasm. Rommel still had not told him what his mission was going to be. 'But it is also a costly means of attack, sir,' he said, his voice without emotion. 'Two of the six downed and perhaps another two severely damaged. Some thirty to sixty percent casualties and the loss of two highly trained pilots who can't be replaced that easily.'

'But if the stakes are high enough, Greim,' Rommel objected. 'If they had have knocked me or my headquarters out, which fortunately they did not, it would have well been worth the loss of those pilots and planes, don't you agree?'

Greim did not answer. He could see that Rommel had been convinced even further by the surprise French raid of the effectiveness of the dive-bomber.

'What might take a regiment of infantry, and all support weapons, some three thousand men, say, all day to achieve, a squadron of Stukas could do in an hour. Don't you think that is worth the losses in men and material, Major?'

Greim took the plunge, as Rommel turned and made his way to the stairs, still shaking his head as if in admiration for the French dive-bombers. 'Sir, you have still not told me the objective for my Squadron?'

Rommel turned, his face hard now. He crooked a finger at the Major. 'Yes,' he said very deliberately, 'I suppose you ought to know as soon as possible. Let us go down to the map-room. I have something to show you…'

Major Greim followed, his heart beating with sudden excitement and apprehension…

BOOK 2: *THE BRIDGE AT GMÜND*

CHAPTER 1

'The gorge of the River Sauer running the length of the Luxembourg-German frontier,' Major Greim announced, tapping the big map with his pointer. 'Our today's objective.'

Outside the sun was already a red ball glimpsed through the wavering grey clouds, beginning to burn away the night's fog rapidly. It would be another sweltering day. 'Well-wooded on both banks, with the hills on either side almost clifflike.'

'*Los … los!*' the crew chiefs outside urged on their men, 'put some shitting pepper in yer pants!' Officers and noncoms were shouting everywhere, as blue-overalled mechanics rushed about to carry out the preparations for the new op, all thought of the twenty-four-hour stand-down forgotten now. Armourers appeared at the double, screw-drivers gripped in their teeth, long belts of gleaming yellow ammunition dangling from their shoulders. Radio-fitters were working furiously at the sets, changing crystals, testing reception, oxygen bottles were being trundled up and heaved above the Stukas. Petrol was being pumped into tanks. All was controlled, hectic chaos.

'Now here,' Greim tapped the map again, purposefully keeping his voice low and unemotional, 'is the hamlet of Gmünd on the German side of the river, a handful of farm cottages climbing up the cliff. With here, on the Luxembourg side, the main riverbank road to Vianden and south, while here on the heights — again on the Luxembourg side — the main south-north axis from France to Belgium…'

Only the dour fanatic Baron Karst listened with any real interest. The others were too tired still or too bored. Obviously they took this for yet another routine mission of the kind they had been flying ever since the campaign had started. Hanno von Heiter played with his tiger cub. Furst Schwarz buffed his lacquered carefully manicured nails, while de la Mazière kept shooting lazy glances out of the window of the briefing hut with bored curiosity.

'Wait, my little friends,' Greim told himself grimly as he continued his lecture. 'You'll sit up in a minute all right, never shittingly well fear!'

'Now, gentlemen,' he continued, 'this is absolutely top-secret, completely confidential,' he swung his gaze around their bored young faces, 'General Rommel will take the strongest measures against anyone mentioning this matter outside of this room. The Führer himself has declared it *Top Secret* in order to stop any panic.'

That did it. Their heads shot up as one. Suddenly there was excitement and eagerness in their weary eyes. Greim let them wait, torturing them a little for their behaviour previously. Outside the first Stuka started to whine and cough and puff like a chronic smoker coming to life first thing in the morning, as the crew turned its reluctant, dawn-cold engine. Far off there was the faint thump-thump of flak.

'Gentlemen, the French have thrown a bridge across the Sauer at Gmünd. At this very moment as I talk to you, there are French soldiers on the soil of the Reich, a mere fifty-sixty kilometres from here.'

His announcement had the effect of a bomb-shell. Karst sprang to his feet, face ashen, fists clenched angrily. De la Mazière cried, 'Oh, no!' Even the Austrian playboy Furst Schwarz was shocked. He dropped his buffer. As for 'Churchill', he disappeared between his master's knees, tail between his legs. 'But there is worse to come,' Greim continued, rubbing it in now. 'Intelli gence has informed General Rommel that the French are changing their armoured tactics after the last few days. Instead of attacking in battalion or company strength as they have done hitherto, they are assembling two whole divisions of armour in the style of our own army, one of them being led by a certain Colonel de Gaulle, an acknowledged French expert in the field of armoured warfare. So you can guess what they are going to do with that damned bridgehead at Gmünd.'

'Yes indeed,' Baron Karst snarled, eyes blazing with rage. 'Striking up from the Metz region they will cross with their armour and hit Rommel — er General Rommel's flank, sir.'

'Worse,' Greim snapped, rubbing their arrogant young noses even deeper in the dirt now, taking a strange kind of pleasure in seeing these ever-so confident SS officers writhe at last. 'Not only General Rommel's, but the whole of the armoured corps. We have denuded our defences along the West Wall. What is left, is only second-rate infantry. If the French manage to launch a major armoured thrust across the Sauer into the flank of our armoured troops, well,' he shrugged. 'All I can say is the immortal words of Sergeant Hanneman: then we will definitely be right up to our hooters in shit!'

A deathly silence greeted his announcement, broken only by the thump-thump of light anti-aircraft guns in the far distance. It seemed Bitburg was being attacked from the air, but the news he had just given them was so startling that they were unable to register that fact.

Greim cleared his throat. If the enemy were bombing Bitburg, it meant they were preparing the ground for a breakout from the Gmünd bridgehead. Time was running out. 'Now, gentlemen,' he continued hurriedly, 'we have been asked by General Rommel to destroy that bridge. It won't be easy,' he warned hurriedly. 'Indeed it will be damnably difficult. Our troops facing the enemy there tell us that the French have positioned flak on both sides of the river on the heights in several kilometres' depth. Then the bridge is hidden by the curve of the valley. So in order to pin-point the damned thing accurately, we shall have to come in exceedingly low and run the gauntlet of their flak, naturally. And one other thing, we must attack from the Luxembourg side of the river. Gmünd is still inhabited by some hundred or so German nationals. We can't run the risk of killing some of our own fellow citizens. Clear?'

'Clear,' they answered as one.

'All right. Karst, you will go in first. Von Heiter, you will follow. Then Schwarz. Finally you, de la Mazière.'

De la Mazière made a gesture as if pulling a lavatory chain, sinking slowly in his chair as he did so. 'Of course, when *I* go,' he said with a hollow chuckle, 'they will all be waiting for me. I'll be presenting myself to the Frogs on a silver platter.'

''Fraid so,' Greim said and Hanno von Heiter laughed and commented, 'You'll make a handsome corpse, de la Mazière.'

'All right,' Greim said, 'In and out as quickly as you can. If enemy fighters attack, form a defensive circle, with ten degrees of flap and keep turning. Your gunners will have to do the best they can. If you are alone, beat it to the nearest cloud cover. Otherwise you haven't a chance. Their fighters are a good one hundred kilometres an hour faster than you. Any questions?'

As usual it was Hanneman.

'Yes Hanneman?' Greim asked, guessing what was coming, for he could always rely on the Old Head to break the tension.

'How soon does my mother get my pension?'

No one laughed and Hanneman muttering an obscenity under his breath relapsed into a sulky silence.

'There is just one more thing,' Greim hesitated, for he knew the effect of what he was going to do next would have on his young fanatics. But Rommel had given him a direct order and he knew why. Rommel wanted his pilots to give their utmost, even if it were at the cost of their young lives. 'I have a message from the Führer to read to you,' he said at last, pulling the paper from the breast pocket of his flying suit.

There was a startled gasp.

Deliberately Greim unfolded the paper and cleared his throat, while the Black Knights stared up at his craggy lined face, as if mesmerized, as if trying to burn every single wrinkle and fold onto their mind's eye.

'Soldiers of the First SS Stuka Squadron. Your hour of trial has come. You are about to execute a task upon which the whole future of the campaign in the West might depend. Destroy that bridge! Sweep the enemy from the sacred soil of the Reich! Cost what it may, I am depending upon you. Soldiers … comrades, I, your Leader Adolf Hitler, salute you!'

As one the young officers sprang to their feet, heels clicking to attention, bodies rigid, as they flung out their arms, faces glowing, eyes burning with almost unbearable fanaticism. '*Heil Hitler!*' their harsh cry filled the room, drowning even the hammering of the flak down in Bitburg.

Greim's heart sank. It was everything Göring had warned about — and worse. Now the Black Knights would go to their deaths gladly, almost gratefully for hadn't their Leader himself urged them to do so. His shoulders bent, as if in defeat, he walked to the door and the waiting Stukas, their engines already beginning to stutter into noisy life.

CHAPTER 2

Below the border country unfolded like a magic carpet. All seemed so peaceful, so tranquil: the dark mass of the fir forests, the two tone checker-board of the meadows and fields, the tiny white villages of the Ardennes clinging to the hillsides as if glued there. It seemed hardly possible that down there, savage half-wild men lurked ready to spring at each other's throats in deadly combat at a moment's notice.

Bringing up the rear of the tight Squadron box, de la Mazière felt a heady sensation of elation sweep over him, as he remembered the Führer's words, and his hands trembled visibly, as he carried out his routine tasks on the panel in front of him. Now they were not merely flying artillery, knocking out obscure, nameless enemy positions. Now they were carrying out a mission of vital importance for the nation. For a few moments he felt like his ancestor Cornet Detlev de la Mazière, after whom he was named, who had seized the regimental flag of the Prussian Guards from the dying senior cornet at St Privat in 1870 and had rallied the men. He had died at their head five minutes later, shot through the heart, but the enemy position had been taken.

Now he felt on top of his form. His eyes were keen, his every muscle firm and ready; for excitement and elation had keyed them up to the highest pitch of efficiency. All fear and apprehension had vanished. He was ready for anything.

Behind him Slack Arse Schmidt tightened his safety straps, changed his position for the umpteenth time and swung the machine gun round the circle, pleased with its well-oiled, easy movement. But that wasn't the only thing he was pleased with.

This mission was going to be a beaut, he knew it; all the peasants did. Before they had climbed into the planes, Hanneman had shaken his hand with unusual formality and said, his voice gruff but somehow emotional, 'Well old horse, I'll stroke my hairy ass, but this one could well be an Ascension Day. Look after yourself and keep yer glassy orbs to the rear — and on that young hot-shot of yours. See he doesn't do anything stupid.' Slack Arse swallowed hard at the memory and wished he'd smuggled a flatman aboard after all. They flew on.

Now the Squadron curved south west, observing strict radio silence for Major Greim assumed that the bridgehead at Gmünd was so important that the French would employ fighters to defend it. He was running no risk of their scrambling their planes at Metz or Étain to meet him. Stukas were sitting ducks for fighters. Flying in front and slightly above the neat box of his Squadron, he swayed back and forth, waggling his wings apparently nervously — but in reality to put any enemy fighter hurtling straight from the sun off his aim — constantly flashing a look at his rear-view mirror. A fighter pilot who didn't do that, didn't live long.

It was perfect bombing weather. Not a cloud in sight, with the burning yellow sun illuminating every feature of the terrain below, now that the last of the fog had been burned away. But it was also a flak-gunner's dream weather. Today there was no hiding place in the sky for an attacking plane. The gunners waiting for them could hardly miss. Their only chance was surprise and speed of attack. In and out within five minutes before the French fighters pounced upon them.

The Sauer came into view. A glittering silver snake meandering along the tight gorges. He sucked in his breath and came lower. The Stukas did the same. He flashed a look to left and right. The heights were perfectly empty. Not a soul in sight. He fell even lower, leaving the squadron above him, black hawks silhouetted clearly against the burning blue wash of the perfect sky. He flicked off his safety catch, huddled deeper down in his seat and shifted his feet on the rudder bar. Now Karst was left in charge of the squadron. He was on his own.

He increased his speed. He judged that at this speed he'd see the bridge within the next minute. Now he was going full throttle, the firs marching up the sides of the river valley hurtling by at a tremendous rate until they merged into one constant dark-green blur. Dark running figures appeared on the heights to his right. Something flashed crimson. A sudden brown puff of smoke disfigured the perfect blue. Now he was *below* the crest, chasing forward at 400 kilometres an hour. A pontoon bridge, heavy with dark figures, like trails of ants, moving to the other side. Lights winked on both sides. It was like the flames of a myriad blast furnaces. Dazzling light filled the sky. Abruptly the air on both sides of him was peppered with angry balls of black smoke. Tracer raced in furious curves towards him. Guns were firing from the trees everywhere. The whole valley seemed aflame. He opened the throttle even wider. Now he was going all out, the flak chasing him, hanging on to his tail.

Bang ... bang! He felt the Messerschmitt reel under the impact. There was the sudden stink of molten metal. For one nightmarish second he thought he had lost control of the plane. Abruptly his throat was full of hot thick green bile. He was sick with fear. And then he had the fighter again. Behind him the bridge disappeared in the gorge and he was climbing desperately, hanging onto the prop, as the damaged fighter soared upwards into the blinding blue, hoping against hope that his desperate ruse had worked and that his bold young fanatics could get in and out before the flak turned its attention to them. A minute later he was a black dot in the blue.

Karst flung a glance to left and right. The smoke clouds were already beginning to disperse in the faint breeze. Men were running about everywhere below. As yet, however, the flak had not opened up again. Greim had prepared the way well. He started to zig-zag and change height to put the gunners off their aim, getting into position for the great attack. Already he could see the headlines blazing a bright scarlet from the front page of the Nazi newspaper, *Völkischer Beobachter*. There would be the Knight's Cross. Perhaps even the Leader himself would hand him the coveted decoration. What a triumph that would be!

Now the bridge was clearly outlined against the silver of the Sauer and it was still packed with the hated French, who were daring to defile the scared soil of the Reich with their decadent, degenerate presence. Karst's lips curled angrily and his eyes flashed fire. 'Lion One to all,' he broke radio silence, thus disobeying Major Greim's specific order, but what did he care? Even if he died in the attempt to destroy the bridge, it would be worth it. Suddenly he felt the Führer himself watching him like some God on high, 'we *attack*!'

The next instant he fell out of the sky, sirens screaming, engine howling. Frantically, down below the French gunners turned their attention to this new threat, swinging their long cannon around in a frenzy of fear and apprehension. Brown and black puff-balls started to fleck the blue on all sides.

Karst did not care. He was carried away by a wild ecstasy that was almost sexual. As he altered his angle of dive from seventy to eighty and then to ninety degrees, he laughed out loud to himself like a crazy man. Behind him Sergeant Hanneman cursed and cursed again at his luck of being crewed with such a madman. He looked back and saw the white blur of the second pilot's face only metres away. 'Fuck off,' he called, although he knew the dive-crazed second pilot couldn't hear him. 'Fuck off, or you'll ram us in a minute!'

But neither Karst nor the rest of his Black Knights cared about such things. Flak filled the air. Tracer flew everywhere. It mattered not. They were out to save Germany. It was their holy task, imposed on them by the beloved Leader himself. Down and down they came. Now everything spun into perspective. The pontoon bridge, the straggle of cottages climbing up the bank on the German side, the flak guns pounding away on both sides, with the larger number positioned on the Luxembourg bank, soldiers running furiously for their lives, some diving over the sides of the bridge into the shallow water.

Karst grunted. The bridge was well centred in his sights. But he mustn't drop any lower. If he did, he might well be destroyed by his own bombs. Behind him, Hanneman in a paroxysm of sudden fear, instinctively knowing what the madman at the stick was going to do, screamed desperately, 'Don't hit the brakes, sir! DON'T —'

Too late. Karst hit the brake rudder. The flaps below the wings came down. The Stuka seemed to stagger in mid-air, a perfect target for the gunners below. Hanneman sweated. They were sitting on a powder keg. Karst didn't care. His sweat-lathered face broke into a cruel grin of triumph. Now, with his speed reduced like this, he couldn't miss. He could already hear the wild roar of the crowds as he rode in an open tourer to meet the Führer to receive his Knight's Cross. He pressed the bomb release in the same instant that a wild explosion to port slammed the Stuka fifty metres to the side as if it had been punched by a gigantic fist. Next moment, the bombs were whistling down and a cursing furious Karst was tugging at his stick, knowing already that he had missed…

Now it was Von Heiter's turn. From high above, circling around like hawks in a defensive circle, de la Mazière and his flight could see the flight of the Squadron's comedian prepare for the run-in. Below fires were burning everywhere. Great mounds of fresh brown earth had appeared on both banks, though miraculously the German hamlet had not been touched. Bodies lay sprawled on all sides like bundles of abandoned rags. But the bridge was still intact and the flak, especially the guns on the Luxembourg side which had the best view, were thudding away constantly. De la Mazière bit his bottom lip as Von Heiter waggled his wings, the signal for the attack. 'Good luck, Hanno,' he whispered. Behind him Slack Arse shook his head, as if in total disbelief.

Hanno fell from the sky. One after the other, the rest of his flight did the same. The wild helter-skelter had commenced yet again. Immediately the French gunners concentrated their fire on the planes hurtling down at an impossible angle, bunched so close together that it seemed they had to crash into one another at any moment. Shell bursts submerged the four planes. The air was full of red explosions and hard black smoke, as if some giant were peppering the sky with lumps of coal. On and on the guns thundered. Down and down the planes raced. It seemed impossible that anyone would survive that tremendous awesome barrage.

De la Mazière, watching that tremendous ride of the Valkyries, groaned suddenly. Von Heiter's number two had been hit. He could see him stagger as the fire ball exploded at his port wing. Desperately the pilot tried to right his stricken plane. To no avail. His port wing went fluttering down, turning over and over, first black then pale blue, like a multicoloured leaf. Immediately the Stuka fell right through the diving formation, engine screaming all out. A flak crew scrambled madly for safety. The Stuka smashed right through the gun, trailing thick black smoke behind it. De la Mazière, hands gripping his controls wet with sweat, willed him to make it. But that wasn't to be. The Stuka's undercarriage hit the cliff-side and snapped like match-wood. Next moment it was hurtling along with the tremendous wake of dust and rock racing behind it to smash head first into a huge boulder. A second later it disintegrated in a great ball of violet flame. Von Heiter's attack had failed. The bridge at Gmünd was still intact and the first of the Black Knights had been killed in action.

'Tiger One — to all,' de la Mazière rasped into his throat mike. 'We're going in as low as we can. Then dive. *Verstanden?*' He didn't wait for their answer, but cut the radio immediately. Perhaps this way he could put the flak off its aim; for the French gunners knew there was still one flight to come.

Now they were some three thousand metres above the Sauer. Down below the cherry-red flashes of the exploding guns indicated that the French gunners were already preparing for the new attack. It didn't worry de la Mazière — yet. At this range they couldn't be too accurate. He started to come lower bringing his flight in on the German side of the river where the flak seemed thinner. Behind him Slack Arse Schmidt tensed at his machine-gun feeling absolutely useless and very vulnerable.

The flight dropped another thousand metres. Now the shells were exploding all around them. Schmidt told himself the flak concentrations around Barcelona in that last fatal attack in 1939 had not been as thick as this. Suddenly he felt paralysed with fear, that agonizing physical fear which twists the guts and fills the mouth with bitter gall. It had been the same then, when he'd seen the C.O.'s plane hit and go trailing off into the countryside, streaming thick black smoke behind it, and he had known that all was lost.

Grimly de la Mazière prepared to attack. It could be no more shitting dangerous down there than up here, he told himself. The sooner he got on with the deadly business, the better. He waggled his wings and flashed one last look in his mirror at the flight. They were racked in right behind him, not more than ten metres separating each plane. He nodded his approval and felt a glow of pride. Nothing could stop men like that, the cream of the Armed SS. The Black Knights were invincible!

He started to depress the stick. Behind him his flight did the same. In a minute twelve tons of fighting fury would rush to the attack — and this time, de la Mazière promised himself grimly, the damned bridge *would* be destroyed, even if he had to sacrifice his life to do so.

'Sir,' Slack Arse Schmidt yelled, 'twelve o'clock high… Moranes, I think!'

De la Mazière flung a look up into the burning sky, narrowing his eyes to slits against the fierce glare of the sun. He groaned. There was no mistaking them. A whole squadron of the French fighters lining up in the sun, obviously readying for the attack. The flak gunners below had called for help. He had to make a split second decision. Up here they would be easy meat for the French. Dive-bombing was impossible too. What was he to do?

'Tiger One — to all,' he cried over the RT, 'jettison … jettison!' the command choked him, even as he gave it, but he knew there was no use sacrificing his flight needlessly. He tugged at his own release and his 250 pounders hurtled towards the ground, purposelessly. The plane surged forward now lightened of its load, as the Moranes completed their form-up and prepared to attack. There was not a moment to be lost. Only speed and surprise could save the flight now. 'Form up on me — line abreast!' de la Mazière rasped. 'Gunners, regular bursts to left and right when I give the command. Let's go! *Los!*'

He fell out of the sky into that dread valley. Almost immediately the French gunners took up the challenge, while the Moranes came skimming down.

'All right, gunners,' de la Mazière said, trying to keep his voice calm, 'the dance has commenced. *Fire!*'

Behind him Schmidt swinging his machine-gun round to face the Luxembourg bank of the river laughed out loud in delight. 'Very smart, sir! Their own fighters won't venture into this little dance-hall.' He pressed the trigger and sent a stream of red tracer into the nearest flak position, flinging the screaming gunners from their perches, arms and legs waving frantically as if they were demented.

Now the four Stukas were flying lower than the flak positions, the soldiers firing at them with rifles and machine guns from the river itself clearly visible, while the Moranes skimmed around above their own flak, suddenly helpless.

Schmidt saw a group of gunners running for a twin flak cannon located near a wooden shed. He fired a controlled burst, walking the slugs along the ground towards the shed. Shreds of wood splinters ripped the length of the place. With absolute clarity he saw how one of the loaders collapsed, the shell tumbling from suddenly nerveless fingers, while another clawed the air in mortal agony, as if he were climbing the rungs of an invisible ladder.

Shrapnel rapped the Stuka's fuselage like the beak of some great hawk, but now the fire was mostly small arms, for the gunners on the heights could not depress their cannon low enough to fire at these impudent daredevils in their gull-winged planes.

But de la Mazière and the other pilots had no time for the ground fire. The ground and hills on both sides raced by at a tremendous speed. It needed absolute total concentration to avoid the obstacles which were everywhere. One wrong move and they would crash. The bridge flashed by, its surface littered with dead bodies but still intact; and then they were swinging around the bend in the gorge and leaving the noise and smoke of battle behind. They had done it. But the bridge at Gmünd was still intact...

CHAPTER 3

'With effect from 17.00 HRS, the notice read, there will be no further mention of flak or the so-called "Flak Valley" in this mess. Any infringement of this order will be punished. Signed W. Greim, Major, *Luftwaffe*', A glum de la Mazière read the new order pinned on the mess notice board, a half-empty glass of beer in his hand.

To his right one of the squadron painters was perched on a ladder carefully painting in the first name on the Squadron's *Roll of Honour*, It seemed so very small and somehow lonely on that large board, he thought. Yet there would be more to come before this bloody business at Gmünd was finished, he knew instinctively.

Behind him an angry Karst, his head bandaged and padded where he had banged it against his cockpit, was saying, 'But time is of the essence. We can't allow the French build-up to continue much longer, comrades. Once they bring up those armoured divisions the C.O. told us about and start sending them across the Sauer, there will be hell to pay.'

'Especially now when Rommel and the rest of the armoured divisions' commanders have committed their men on the other side of the Meuse,' Schwarz said, seated at the piano, though this evening the lid remained closed. He was too weary and too shaken by the events of that day to play. De la Mazière frowned. They were all beat. Since the morning they seemed to have aged. Their faces appeared white and drawn, with circles beneath the blood-shot eyes, almost as if they had lost weight, a lot of it, in a matter of a few hours. He noticed too the nervous tic at the left side of Karst's face and the way he kept taking his monocle out and then screwing it back in again.

'The C.O. told me before dinner that he was attempting to obtain a squadron of fighters from a pal of his at the Air Ministry. If he can, they'll be sent in first. We'll follow. And Met says there'll be early morning fog.' He shrugged a little weakly. 'Perhaps that'll give us a bit of cover,' de la Mazière added without much conviction.

Only Karst still had the strength to react, 'But there are still those damned —' he flashed a glance at the new order '— you-know-whats on the heights waiting for us to come down out of the fog. Fighters ... fog ... all well and good. But what about the you-know-whats?'

But no one had the answer to that particular overwhelming question.

Schwarz rose with a weary sigh. '*Meine Herren,*' he yawned. '*Servus,* I shall now recline my alabaster torso on my four poster and seek the boon of Morpheus.'

No one laughed. Karst nodded, again taking out his monocle almost angrily and screwing it back into his eye again, 'Yes, Schwarz is right. We all need as much sleep as we can get — for the morrow, *Gute Nacht meine Herren.*'

Idly de la Mazière wandered outside the Mess. He felt exhausted, but somehow he didn't think he could sleep just yet. Besides it was still very warm, with hardly a breath of air stirring across the darkening field. He stood there, breathing in the humid air, staring at the dark high shapes of the Stukas, already fuelled and re-ammunitioned for the morrow, their bullet-ripped and shredded sides hastily repaired by the aircraft fitters. They would fly at dawn. He frowned, and wondered what the morrow would bring in that terrible valley of the

River Sauer, which they were already calling among themselves 'Flak Valley'.

'De la Meziere,' the familiar voice broke into his reverie.

He swung round. It was Hanno von Heiter. He was flushed and worried.

'What is it, Hanno?'

'Have you seen Churchill?'

For one minute de la Mazière hadn't the faintest idea what his comrade was talking about. Then he remembered. The tiger cub. 'No,' he said. 'What's wrong?'

'I can't find the damned beast anywhere. He's vanished. He wasn't here when we came back from the attack.'

De la Mazière was tempted to say that one of the peasants might already have him in a pot. They were reputed to be able to eat anything, even the tinned 'Old Man' ration meat, supposedly made from the bodies of old men in Berlin's many workhouses. But he caught himself in time. Hanno was too attached to his mascot. 'Perhaps he got out of your quarters and hopped it onto the field,' he suggested. 'You know how playful he is.'

'Yes, that might be it,' von Heiter agreed, brightening up for a moment, then his gloom returned. 'I've got to find him, de la Mazière. He's my mascot.' He bit his bottom lip. 'I can't fly without him… He's my luck, you know. It would be bad…' He didn't finish the rest of his sentence.

He didn't have to. De la Mazière knew what he meant. All of them had some sort of mascot or talisman that they thought in the superstitious manner of pilots brought them luck and protected them from danger. He suspected that Karst's monocle was his. 'Shall I help you look, Hanno?'

'No, no, I've got to do that myself. But I *must* find him before we fly! I *must*!' There was a note of despair in the other pilot's voice. 'Good night, de la Mazière,' he said hastily and darted away into the growing darkness, leaving de la Mazière to stare after his tall lean form until he vanished into the gloom. Only then did de la Mazière turn and walk slowly back to his own quarters, trying to fight off his growing mood of apprehension and disquiet.

The mood was no better in the Sergeants' Mess that night. Everywhere the air gunners, most of them still in their stained, torn flying suits in spite of the oppressive heat, were slumped at the beer-stained trestle tables, surrounded by the crew chiefs, who watched their comrades furtively, saying little; knowing the hell the air gunners must have been through this day. Hadn't they worked all that long spring evening patching up the bullet-holed, torn fabric of the Stukas?

'Was it as bad as it looked — from the crates, I mean?' Papa Dierks ventured. He looked at Schmidt sitting next to a gloomy Hanneman, his unshaven face buried in his mug. 'Bad,' Schmidt echoed the query with a hollow laugh. 'Bad ain't the word for it. It was *shitting, crapping awful!* I could have filled my skivvies a good dozen times over.'

'They went at it like Blücher at Waterloo,' Hanneman agreed mournfully, raising his head at last. 'You should have seen the black bastards. You would have thought that old Adolf himself had been down there at the bridge, handing Knight's Crosses out by the basketful, the way they charged at it. Thank God for those frog fighters, comrades, or Mrs Hanneman's handsome son wouldn't have been sitting here at this very minute supping lukewarm suds that taste like horse's piss.' He took an angry swig of his beer. 'Still, one of the arrogant black bastards went hop this afternoon if that's any consolation.'

'But young de la Mazière,' Schmidt said slowly, 'he wasn't too bad. He did get us out of the mess very nicely in the end. You've got to admit that, Hanneman.'

The big red-faced sergeant wasn't impressed. 'So,' he shrugged contemptuously, 'what am I supposed to do, Slack Arse, shoot my wad in gratitude? He got us out of the shit today, but he'll probably have us right in it up to our hooters tomorrow morning. He's no different from the rest, believe you me.' He looked at the faces of his fellow NCOs, hollowed out to death's heads in the growing gloom, not speaking for a moment, the only sound the buzz of the mosquitoes. 'Listen,' he said finally, 'as long as that crapping bridge stands, our poor peasant heads are on the chopping block. All that concerns them is glory, even if they have to go and get their stupid turnips blown off in the attempt. I tell you, comrades,' he finished with a weary sigh, 'buy combs, there are lousy times ahead.' He stumbled to his feet, not even finishing the rest of his beer, something very unusual for Sergeant Hanneman, who was famed throughout the old regular *Luftwaffe* as a notorious sauce-hound, 'Comrades, I'm gonna sling my ear at the hay. But mind what I say,' he finished darkly, 'buy combs, there are lousy times ahead…'

Major Greim dreamed. He was back in that blazing Stuka over Barcelona, his radial engine spluttering frighteningly, glycol spurting over the shattered cockpit, the pain in his shattered arm almost unbearable, desperately trying to land the crippled plane outside the Red capital; for he knew well what would happen if the Loyalists caught him. A clean death by firing squad would be a boon. On all sides the rest of the Squadron were streaming down, trailing black smoke behind them, to their destruction.

Somehow he had managed it. He had escaped the sprawling Catalonian city and its fanatical defenders, who were reputed to castrate their prisoners and put out their eyes, and staggered out beyond the lush coastal belt to belly-land in one of the remote mountain valleys of the Pyrenees.

Twenty-four hours later he had come to again in the cave, his skull fractured and several ribs cracked in addition to his bullet-shattered arm, to find Conchita, all flashing teeth and liquid-black worried eyes, tending him. He had croaked in his pathetic kitchen Spanish, 'Am I a prisoner?' She had shaken her head and pressed another wet compress to his forehead and he had slipped into unconsciousness once more.

Weeks passed, and he started to grow well and strong again, tended by the Spanish girl and her son, Miguel, a bright-eyed lively boy in spite of the poor food on which they lived. By day Conchita would disappear, while the boy looked after him bringing him water and fruit, teaching and correcting him, but always wary and on guard, dark eyes afraid, whenever there was an unusual sound outside the cave where they hid him; for as he explained there were still wandering bands of the '*Rojos*' in the mountains everywhere and the 'reds' would do *cosas terribles* to him and '*mamita*' if they ever discovered they were hiding a 'Franco man'. In the evening she would return, bringing with her a hunk of bread, some vegetable, occasionally a bottle of *tinto* or a skinny yellow Spanish chicken.

Greim had never asked where and how she had got the food, but he could guess. He had been long enough in Spain to know the fierce moral code of that remote country. Conchita with her flashing eyes, olive skin and slim figure was not from here; she was from the city. Her hands were not work-worn like those of the normal sturdy, bow-legged peasant woman. They were still soft and shapely and they bore no wedding ring on the middle finger of the left hand, although Conchita had a son whom she loved tenderly. Conchita was a 'fallen woman', in Spanish eyes, a woman with a child and no husband. Now all men — and most of their women, too, for that matter — would regard her, especially in the countryside, as a *'chica libre'*, a 'free girl', a prostitute in other words. So he could guess how a penniless woman, hiding in this barren cave, which was her only home apparently, found the food with which she fed him and her son.

Once when they had all three hidden in the back of the cave for a whole day from a marauding patrol of Red cavalrymen who were rampaging through the district plundering, burning, raping, indulging themselves in one last mad orgy of destruction before they fled over the mountains to surrender to the French (for the Republic was about finished and Franco had already taken Barcelona), she had whiled away the time by telling him stories of Spain. She had related the old tales of the Jews and the Gypsies, the 'Moors,' as she called the Arabs who had occupied the country for nearly a thousand years, and the *'cristianos'* who had reconquered it back from them.

By chance (or was it?, he had often asked himself later) she had told him of the *comprachicos*, the 17th century gypsy band called the 'boy buyers', who bought three-year-old children from poverty-stricken parents. Then the 'boy buyers' started to work systematically on the little innocents. They applied metal braces to stunt and bend their frail limbs. They used knives and red-hot wires to turn their faces into grotesque masks and had hung their legs with heavy weights to stop the normal rate of infant growth. And then when a few years of this terrible perverted torture had had their effect, they had sold these Frankensteins to royal courts and travelling circuses — even zoos — for a handsome profit. There, these dwarfs with their horrid, frightening faces and deformed limbs lived their short lives of unbelievable misery and pain to amuse the rich and the powerful until mercifully an early death released them.

After that story she had grown silent and had looked at the little boy Miguel sleeping on a pile of potato sacks at the rear of the cave, with eyes full of fear and infinite compassion. Greim had understood. That night for the first and last time he took her and afterwards as he had soothed her tears and hushed her confessions, he had sworn a terrible oath. Whatever came in the future, he would survive and ensure that Conchita and Miguel never came to harm. The *comprachicos* would never come for the son of the woman who had saved him. *Never!* Now as Major Greim tossed and turned in his sweat-soaked bunk, the mosquitoes humming everywhere in the stifling blacked-out room and the bats wheeling and screeching outside as they had done in the cave that night she had told him that terrible story, he was tormented with visions of Miguel, terrible visions, which made him groan and moan in his sleep.

The *comprachicos* had placed Miguel in a porcelain vase, designed with nightmarish cunning to twist and pervert his growth. Only the top and bottom of the jar had been left open so that Miguel's head and feet had been free for imaginative sadistic surgery. Now the swarthy-faced grinning gypsies had broken open the vase and out of it as from some monstrous cocoon — had crawled an unbelievable horror.

It squatted there on the floor, panting, like a dog, just barely recognizable as Miguel. Its lopsided face was twisted to one side, one eye staring upwards at an impossible angle, the other staring at him, full of dark knowing cunning. Slowly, very slowly, it began to raise one of those tiny limp arms like those of a six month old foetus, and beckon to him. Behind him

Conchita's face, olive-brown and lovely, in spite of the tears streaming down her cheeks, appeared ghost-like and disembodied from the wavering mist which surrounded the monster lolling there on the floor, the grotesque mask set in an inane toothless grin. '*Walter...*' the voice seemed to come from eons of time away, echoing and re-echoing down the gloomy awesome corridors of eternity, '*Walter ... querido mio ... help us ... help us ... help ... he...*' There was such an infinity of sadness and need in that echoing cry that in his dream he felt his eyes flood with tears and his heart begin to bleed for them and their absolute overwhelming misery...

'Sir!' he felt his shoulder clutched hard. He woke with a start, his heart thudding crazily, his pyjamas soaked with hot sweat. 'Four o'clock, sir!' the harsh voice of the duty sergeant snapped, blinding Greim with his torch. 'Time to get up, sir!'

'Thanks ... thank you, Sergeant,' Greim stuttered. 'All right, I'm awake now.'

'Thank you, sir.' The NCO ticked his name off the roster attached to his clipboard and stamped out in his heavy boots.

Greim lay there, panting, as if he had just run a great race, feeling the beads of sweat trickling down his chest unpleasantly. With difficulty he drove the thoughts of that nightmare from his mind. Conchita and Miguel were all right, he knew. He had established them in a little house on the coast near Barcelona, sending them half his Air Force pay, a small fortune in Spain, every month. Miguel was going to school now and Conchita might even find a husband on account of the money now, even though she had once been a '*chica libre*'. If she didn't, then he would bring them both, in spite of the difficulties imposed on such things by the authorities so eager these days to keep the Reich 'racially pure', to Germany. Outside, the first engines started to splutter and cough as the fitters began to warm them up for the battle to come. Reluctantly Greim got out of his bunk and seizing the pail of water, dipped his head into it, coming up, spluttering and gasping for air, that horrid creature on the floor grinning up at him hideously banished from his mind at last. He stared at himself in the little mirror on the dresser, water dripping down his pale face, speaking to himself in the fashion of all lonely men, 'Don't worry the two of you … I shall come back.' Then he forgot them and got on with the bloody business of that day.

CHAPTER 4

The nine yellow-nosed Messerschmitts climbed hard and fast. Below the fog was concentrated in the narrow Ardennes valleys in long milky trails. They flew over the opaque mass dragging their black shadows behind them, while above the sun was so dazzling that the pilots had to lower their smoked glasses. To the front the sky glittered like a molten ingot. Within minutes they were gasping for breath in the stifling cockpits.

At exactly five fifty-two, the squadron leader waggled his wings. Obviously control had guided him to the exact spot. They began to descend gently. For the moment there was no need for full throttle. There wasn't an enemy plane in sight and at this height they had nothing to fear from the flak guns hidden beneath the layers of fog somewhere below. Another minute went by. Now the glittering sun was beginning to disappear and they were slipping perceptibly into the inert, lead-grey mass. Hastily the pilots pushed up their smoked glasses. They had no need of them now. The bright rays no longer pierced their eyes like sharp arrows.

They came lower and lower. Still no cherry-red spurts of flame in the grey which would indicate flak fire. Why? Suspicious now, the fighter pilots began to glance from right to left, punctuating their search with regular looks at the rear-view mirror. Instinctively they broke into a loose untidy formation, zig-zagging from side to side to put any would-be surprise attacker off his aim.

Now they were down to a thousand metres. Here and there, through gaps in the fog they caught fleeting glimpses of the river. They were on target all right. Why were the frogs not firing at them? The pilots looked even harder for the enemy. Left, right, rear, a quick lift of the plane's nose for a better look behind, a swift tilt of the wings to look below.

Still nothing.

Tension mounted. In spite of the fact that it was appreciably colder in the cockpits the pilots still sweated with nervousness and apprehension. What was wrong with the frogs? Suddenly a harsh excited young voice cut into the tense silence, crackling over the RT, 'Bogies at eleven o'clock!'

As one, the young Messerschmitt pilots swung their eyes to the left.

There they were coming silently and somehow sinisterly out of the fog, sliding through the grey waves like multi-coloured sharks.

'Hurricanes!' someone cried excitedly.

'Let's hope they're Belgies. Not Tommies,' another voice yelled. 'Knock it off — the chatter!' the stern voice of the squadron commander broke into the excited to and fro, staring at the approaching aircraft as they came racing now towards the Messerschmitts in a loose scythe shaped formation. 'Hunter Three, going down,' he made his decisions, 'Hunter Two and One — top cover!'

Now the Messerschmitts separated, each to his allotted station, as the two forces approached each other at 400 kilometres an hour. A flight of four German fighters carried out a swift 360 degree turn. There they fanned out to block the Hurricanes' path. The Hurricanes came skimming in unafraid. Suddenly they did a stall turn.

It was the signal for combat.

Now it was every man for himself. Cannon chattered. Tracer flew back and forth in a mad bright criss-cross. Engines snarled as the pilots flung their planes about in the drifting clouds of fog.

Steep climb, half-roll, stick back, the two enemies tried frantically to get into position for the kill. But at the precise moment the one would have the other in his sights he'd skid to the side like a boxer avoiding a straight left. Now it was a question of who would weary first and make a mistake. Round and round they raced in the mad helter-skelter. Exhausts belched blue flame. White contrails ripped through the blue. Multi-coloured tracer zipped back and forth.

A Messerschmitt made the first kill. A Hurricane fell out of the sky, surrounded by spurting white glycol vapour. A hunched figure went whirling through the mad, twisting, turning planes, head tucked well in, hands clasped on tightly crouched legs. A moment after he was clear, he stopped with an abrupt jerk in mid-air and a white parachute blossomed forth from his back.

A Messerschmitt curved in a silver scimitar towards a Hurricane. But there was another enemy plane on his tail. In the excitement of the kill he had failed to check his rearview mirror. He never lived to find out who murdered him. An angry flash. The sword thrust of tracer. Next moment the Messerschmitt had turned on its back like a dog when attacked by a superior opponent. Smoke streamed from its shattered fuselage in a thick pall. It disappeared into the cloud of fog. No one got out.

Down below in the fog Major Greim glimpsed the stabs and spurts of flame vaguely through the opaque shifting grey. It was time for his Black Knights to attack. He pressed his radio switch. 'An *alle*,' he commanded, voice perfectly calm now again, '*angreifen… Attack!*'

They needed no urging.

Coming in over the edge of the cliff-like river bank in broken formation to confuse the gunners, running now to their anti-aircraft cannon, they zoomed upwards through the fog and split, peeling off on all sides like a black tulip opening up. It was exactly as Greim had planned. 'This morning,' he had ordered them, back at Bitburg, 'we don't come in in formation. That'd make it too easy for the French gunners. We want to confuse them, because they feel they know our usual attack formation. This time it will be completely different.' He had frowned with worry. 'Of course I know it's going to be tricky. There'll be a hell of a risk of mid-air collisions, but it's a risk we've got to take. Come in, then, from all sides at irregular intervals. Then drop your eggs and get the hell out of the place — *dalli, dalli.*'

Now gaining height, the first shells already falling towards them through the fog, though instinctively the Stuka pilots knew they had rattled the French gunners, they prepared for the attack, while above them a mad fight to the death raged.

Greim waited, circling between the two formations, waiting for the first French fighter to come lower and spot the new attackers, knowing that this time his losses would be heavy; there could be no doubt of that.

A thick black dot appeared against the grey. He stopped worrying, suddenly tense, nerves jangling electrically. The other plane, growing larger by the instant, started to come in in a spiral dive. It was the standard attack approach. It had to be a Frenchman.

Next moment he recognized the typical silhouette of a Morane. Greim opened the throttle flat out. Throwing the Messerschmitt into a steep climbing turn, he attempted to gain height. The tactic surprised the Frenchman. He opened fire at once, but already his target had gone. The tracer cut the air where Greim had just been, harmlessly. Greim levelled out, feeling gravity slam him back against his armoured seat. He started a tight turn. The Morane tried to turn inside him. His wings would not do it. The Morane stalled and went into a spin. Greim was after him in an instant. They roared lower and lower. Now Greim could see patches of silver glistening through the holes in the fog. It was the Sauer and in a moment his Black Knights would be coming in for the attack, now that they had gained sufficient height. He had to deal with the Morane before that. Even the rankest amateur fighter-pilot could shoot down a Stuka when it was diving.

Now the French pilot had come out of his spin. Aware that Greim was on his tail, he started to hurl the Morane all over the place to throw the German off. Greim hung on grimly, as the Morane drifted into his gun sight. At four hundred metres he hit the button. Quick short controlled bursts — he had to conserve his precious ammunition this day. The Frenchman twisted and turned, trying to outdistance his pursuer. Suddenly he pushed the stick forward. In an instant he roared into a vertical dive. But Greim, the old hand, was not to be shaken off so easily.

At five hundred kilometres an hour they raced downwards. But Greim knew time was running out. One of them would have to level out in a moment or risk smacking nose-first into the earth. He tapped the button three times, one, two, three, barely touching it.

A ripple of red flashes ran the length of the cockpit and engine. Bits of glittering metal flew off. The fuselage shook. Suddenly the Morane's prop stopped turning. White glycol streamed out of the Frenchman's exhausts. The plane was racked by a violent explosion. It was the end. Thick black oily smoke shot from it, followed a second later by the first greedy little flames, licking the length of its fuselage. Greim hung on no longer. The Frenchman hadn't a chance. He had to break before he, too, crashed. He broke sharply to port in the very same instant that the shell exploded just below him. The whole plane was slammed upwards a hundred metres as if lifted by some enormous weight-lifter. Suddenly Greim felt the cold air rushing in everywhere. He had been hit! The engine began to cough and splutter alarmingly. Even in the cockpit he could smell the cloying stench of escaping gasoline. One of his fuel tanks had been ripped apart by shrapnel and his engine had been hit, too. He looked at his gauge. His gas was dropping alarmingly. He bit his bottom lip as more and more black puffballs of smoke peppered the fog all around him, the gunners concentrating on this obvious target. Then he made his decision. He could help his officers no more. He would have to return to base. Now the Black Knights were on their own. Mumbling a prayer for his doomed pilots, he swung the crippled plane round awkwardly, the engine coughing and hiccupping all the time as, gas trailing behind him, he vanished eastwards…

CHAPTER 5

Hanno von Heiter had the impression he was hurtling down into a mad aquarium full of crazy fish, as he came into the attack. Nothing but thundering flak, stabs of scarlet flame, roaring engines, the grey air criss-crossed with contrails and the multicoloured lethal morse of tracer bullets.

He tried to dismiss Churchill from his mind. He had searched for him most of the night before flinging himself exhausted onto his bunk for a brief sleep. Now his head was thick and aching, although he had allowed himself a mighty slug of oxygen from one of the cylinders before he had clambered into his Stuka. He tried to concentrate, but at the back of his mind there was still that nagging fear that the loss of his mascot had induced. To his right, a flak battery had spotted him, as he raced for the bridge at a crazy angle. He swung to port. A salvo of shells missed his plane by metres. *Whew, what a party!* he hissed to himself as he fought to hold the bucking plane steady. In an instant he was soaked with sweat, which ran into his eyes, down his neck, under his armpits — everywhere. He could smell his own stink.

Schwarz raced across his front, appearing from nowhere. He hit the rudder. His plane shuddered again and he saw Furst fall to the right, blue flame shooting out of his exhausts. Below to the right of the bridge, a French fighter — a Morane, he thought — slammed into the cliff-face and exploded in a roaring purple ball of flame, scattering fire everywhere. In an instant the firs were blazing.

Desperately von Heiter tried again. He swung the Stuka down almost to ground level, racing up the slope at the

Luxembourg side, catching the gunners by surprise before they could swing the cannon round to catch him. Next moment he was gone beyond the hills and out of range.

A Messerschmitt roared by trailing smoke. He waved to the pilot, but there was no response. 'Come on, old house,' he called, knowing the other pilot couldn't hear him, 'we who are about to die, salute thee — give us a bit of a smile.' He waved again at the dark blue in the gleaming cockpit.

But there was still no response. The Messerschmitt flew on, with the pilot still slumped there, still and unnatural. Hanno von Heiter shuddered as he felt a cold finger of fear trace its way down his spine. What was wrong? Was the man severely wounded, or too shocked to reply? It was all very eerie. God in heaven, why didn't he have Churchill's comforting fur to stroke at this moment? *Why?*

He began to climb again. Above him the stabs of flame cutting the grey indicated that the great dogfight between the Messerschmitts and the Hurricanes was continuing. Now the fog was beginning to thin out and he could see the first blood-red glint of the sun. He was high enough. He didn't want to emerge into the midst of that mess up there. He straightened up and turned east again.

A Stuka swung out of the gloom, trailing smoke. He had no time to recognize the pilot, but the Stuka told him he was near the bridge again. He flew through the thick black smoke blinded for a moment and then there it was again — that damned bridge at Gmünd.

'All right,' he commanded himself, 'a quick split-arse turn — and here we go!'

Teeth gritted hard, breath coming in harsh gasps, the Squadron's comedian hurled his plane downwards. Half turning on his back, he flung himself round again, hoping against hope that he would throw the gunners off. The bridge loomed larger and larger. As before it was packed tight with vehicles. Men were running everywhere. Others flung themselves over the side into the Sauer and struck out wildly for the bank. A Stuka cut into his vision. One two, three, four, he could see its bombs fall quite clearly. 'Out of the way, you silly bastard!' he called, carried away by the mad excitement of the kill now, 'and let a real pilot get on with it!'

Bombs straddled both sides of the bridge. A tremendous fountain of whirling white water sprang up, reaching a hundred metres. And another ... and another. For a mad second the bridge was obscured. Hanno bit his bottom lip. The unknown pilot had hit the bridge. It was probably Karst. He had all the luck. But when the water had settled again the bridge was still there, though several of the trucks on it were burning fiercely and the other Stuka was fleeing for the cover of the hills, tracer chasing it like a swarm of furious red hornets.

Hanno von Heiter pressed home his attack. Now the bridge was directly centred in his sights. He wouldn't miss now. He *couldn't*. 'All right!' he screamed, his face flattened to a red mask by the centrifugal force, feeling himself glued against the back of his seat as he raced down at ninety degrees, *'take this!'*

Abruptly the shield to his front crumpled into a glittering spider's web. He was blinded instantly. Something wet and warm was trickling down his ashen, sweat-lathered face. For one awful terrifying moment, he thought he had been blinded and screamed out in abject fear. Then he realized what had happened. The canopy had been hit by shrapnel and he was bleeding from face wounds. The wild excitement that had coursed through his veins vanished as soon as it had come. He pressed the bomb release button, knowing it was hopeless to attempt to hit the bridge blind. The Stuka jumped, its load lightened. Angrily, Hanno von Heiter pulled back the stick. The Stuka responded immediately, though already he could smell fire. He turned her on her back and released the canopy. It fluttered away and cold air flooded in, filled with the stink of fuel and smoking grease from overheated systems. He paused and hoped that the 'knicker silk', as they called the parachute, would open. 'It's all your shitting fault,' he cursed, 'you shitting mangy cat. *Curse you, Churchill!*'

Next instant he launched himself into space and raced across the river, huddled in a foetal ball, while below his bombs exploded harmlessly in the Sauer.

Furst Schwarz thought fleetingly of the last plump Rhenish pigeon he had had in Koblenz before the attack. The Romans had left a lot of Latin blood behind them on the Rhine; that little shopgirl *had* really liked it, and he had given her a very thorough snaking. They had danced the mattress polka most of the night and she had wanted it yet once again before breakfast. 'But *mein liebes gnädiges Fräulein,*' he had exclaimed, ' you can't expect a Schwarz to perform without his coffee and croissant, I beg you!' He smiled at the memory. He had caught her after the second cup, just as she was bending over the bed to pour his third. He had made quite a mess of her sheets. Still she had been overjoyed. As he had kissed her hand in his most gallant Viennese cavalier's fashion with his usual '*küss die Hand, gnädiges Fräulein*', she had presented him with a bottle of good Rhenish hock and a packet of sandwiches for the trip back to base and the promise that 'I might have one or two little surprises for you next weekend.' Unfortunately the war and the new campaign in the West had interfered with that weekend. For one moment he wondered what 'little surprises' the plump Rhenish pigeon might have had in store for him. He had thought they had tried most of them out during their nightlong mattress polka together. But one never knew in bed-gymnastics what a woman could do. He blew her an imaginary kiss and whispered in his most seductive Viennese manner, 'Wait for me, my little cheetah. I'll be back next weekend, laden with medals;' then dismissing the little shopgirl, he concentrated on the task at hand, and the business of winning those all-important medals.

Now the fog was beginning to drift away a little and large holes had begun to appear in it as the sun started to burn ever more fiercely. Already he could feel its rays singeing his back and neck. Still there was enough of the fog around to provide him with some cover. He would use it as best he could until he sighted the bridge, through one of the gaps. With a bit of luck he could swoop down the gap in the fog, as if he were rushing down a slide, drop his eggs — right on the damned thing — and be off before the French — what delightful little tricks their women-folk played between the sheets — knew what had happened. His mind was made up.

Humming an indecent little verse to the tune of Strauss's *Wiener Blut*, Furst Schwarz, the last of a long line of Viennese aristocrats, impoverished by a generation-old addiction to fast women and slow horses, went in for the attack…

Baron Karst cursed. 'Those damned guns, Hanneman; those damned guns, Hanneman!'

A sweating Hanneman did not reply. He was too busy swinging his m.g. from left to right, scything the French flak positions, as the Stuka rushed from the river, shells exploding all about it, shrapnel ripping at the fuselage, already shredded here and there to the framework.

Now Karst had attacked three times and three times he had been forced to break off his dive without dropping his bombs, something which worried Hanneman mightily, as the Stuka dropped over the other side of the protecting hill and he ceased firing. Any normal pilot would have dropped them at the first dive, telling himself that the opposition was just too stiff. Not Karst. He was going to plant his eggs on target and cure his throatache this day — or die in the attempt.

'It couldn't happen to a nicer chap,' a little voice inside Hanneman's aching head said cynically, 'but *without* Mrs Hanneman's handsome son.'

Karst throttled back to save fuel, flying along the ridge line slowly, while below the German infantrymen dug in there waved enthusiastically, pointing to the great canvas arrows spread out on the ground, indicating the direction of the enemy positions. Baron Karst took no notice, but Hanneman waved back, saying, 'Don't worry, you stupid, hairy-assed stubble-hoppers, we're not gonna drop our eggs on you. The hotshot I've got up front has got other ideas.'

'Hanneman,' Karst's voice broke into his thoughts.

'Sir?'

'Have you noticed where most of that flak is coming from?'

Hanneman wanted to explode. 'What do you mean, arse with ears! The shit's coming from all sides! Christ on a crutch, what do you think I am, some village dumdum, waiting to hear the wet fart hit the side of the thundermug!' In fact, he said mildly, 'No, sir, I've been too busy with the m.g. to notice.'

'Well, I have,' Karst said in that harsh pedantic manner of his. 'It's coming from the Luxembourg side.'

Below a Messerschmitt was limping back to base, thick black smoke streaming from it, its fabric pocked by shell- and bullet-holes like the symptoms of some loathsome skin disease.

Hanneman puffed out his lips in doubt. The unknown pilot would never make it; he ought to bale out while he still had time.

Karst, pre-occupied with the problem of the bridge, did not seem to notice.

'And I shall tell you something else. Just beyond the village of Gmünd itself on the German side there is one single flak battery. A two hundred and fifty pound bomb on it and the way would be clear, at least from the eastern bank, for a quick run on the bridge.' For one moment Hanneman considered Karst's words, then their full implication struck him like a bomb. 'You mean, knock that battery out and use the remaining three bombs to hit the bridge, sir?' he gasped.

'Exactly.'

'But, sir, there are the civilians, German civilians, in Gmünd. Even if we planted the egg on the flak battery, the exploding ammo around the guns, the shrapnel…'

His breath gave out. 'Sir,' he gasped, 'they are *our* people!'

Karst's voice was icy. 'Peasants, simple backward peasants, probably half of them are not true Germans anyway. One knows this border pack. Even so, one can't make an omelette without breaking eggs. They should be proud to make the sacrifice if it helps to save their Fatherland from the French!'

'But —'

'No more buts, Hanneman,' Karst interrupted harshly, warming to the idea by the instant. 'Of course, it's the only way.' He started to turn the battered Stuka round slowly. Below, the crippled Messerschmitt smashed into the hillside and erupted in a vivid ball of flame with the startling suddenness of a photographer's flash.

Hanneman, veteran that he was of two wars, stared down aghast. Kill their own people... No bridge was worth that.

'*Wiener Blut ... Wiener Blut ... stock hinein, nicht so tief, so ist gut,*' Furst Schwarz sang obscenely, as he circled above the gap in the fog. He was directly above the bridge. It was silhouetted against the foggy sky perfectly, two thousand metres below. Behind him his gunner grinned. Old Schwarz was in good form. Tonight when they landed, he, the gunner, would be richer by twenty marks, for the Prince spent his money generously, especially now when it seemed he was going to destroy the bridge.

'All right,' Furst Schwarz's voice rasped in that nasal Viennese accent of his which reminded the gunner of those stage Austrians who dominated the UFA films. 'I think we'll pay our visit — *now*!' Furst Schwarz tightened his stomach muscles for what was to come. Next instant he flung the stick down. The Stuka fell from the sky. Tracer ripped through the grey fog. He didn't see it. He was falling at 400 kilometres an hour through a chute of fog. A shell exploded to port. The Stuka rocked violently. Schwarz simply laughed. Nothing could stop him now. Down and down he hurtled. The bridge loomed ever larger. He couldn't miss ... he couldn't!

'*Here I come, my plump Rhenish pigeon*!' he shrieked out loud, carried away by a frenzied, crazed, almost sexual excitement, as he positioned his thumb on the bomb release. '*Here I —*' Suddenly a thunderclap. A burning hellish hot slap in the face. His eardrums burst at once. Blood spurted from his nostrils. A hole had abruptly appeared in his windshield. A shell!

Crash!

Another shell slammed into the perspex. His mask full of blood, red and silver stars crackling before his eyes, Furst Schwarz tried to break to the side, the bombing run forgotten now. But that wasn't to be. There would be no more plump Rhenish pigeons for the last of the Schwarzes.

Terrifyingly the wings of the Stuka shuddered as they were ripped apart by the hammer blows of 20mm cannon-fire. Flames spurted up on all sides. He was blinded by a tremendous flash. The rudder fell off. In an instant, the Stuka was completely out of control. Helplessly the crippled plane went into its death dive.

'*Mama*!' Furst Schwarz screamed. '*MAMA...*!'

CHAPTER 6

De la Mazière flung an anxious glance at the gauge showing the Stuka's radiator temperature. It was going up alarmingly. His oil pressure was dropping at the same time.

'What's it like back there, Schmidt?' he rapped, trying to steady the plane, as the shell bursts came closer again, the sky all around him peppered with thick puffballs of evil black smoke.

'I think we've been holed about six times, sir,' Schmidt replied. 'My flippers are freezing. There's air coming in all over the place. Goes on like this and my outside plumbing will have seized up.'

In spite of his tension, de la Mazière smiled. For a peasant, his air gunner had a nice dry sense of humour. 'I think we've had it, Schmidt,' he made his decision. His oil pressure was dropping at an alarming rate. In a minute the big Jumo engine would seize up. Before then, he had to bring the crippled plane down, 'I'm going to have to land.'

Schmidt flung a glance at the ground below, with guns belching fire on all sides and machine-guns filling the burning sky with tracer. 'I think we'd be safer up here, sir,' he quipped.

'Probably,' de la Mazière answered coolly, trying to conceal his chagrin at having to abort yet another damn bombing mission on the damned bridge and his anxiety about what was soon to come. 'Just start praying that our undercarriage hasn't been hit too.' Now he concentrated on the task at hand. He came lower and lower, trailing black oily smoke behind him. Satisfied that another of the hated dive-bombers would soon meet its doom, the French flak-gunners turned their attention to the other Stukas attacking yet once again: something for which de la Mazière was properly grateful; for soon he would have to decelerate from a hundred kilometres an hour to a dead stop in a space of perhaps one hundred metres — that is if he found a suitable piece of road on which to land.

He swooped over the cliff-like river bank. The Sauer and the battlefield disappeared behind him. Suddenly the air was calm, the gunfire vanished. De la Mazière didn't notice. Oil pressure was down to almost zero. It wouldn't be long now. Desperately he searched for a straight stretch of road among the damned firs which seemed to be everywhere. Now the sweat streamed down his back in damp, hot rivulets and his undershirt stuck to his body like a cold wet towel.

Automatically while he searched, his fingers, feeling like sausages, thick and clumsy, found the seat adjustor. He lowered it in order to protect his head in case the plane turned turtle. Behind him Schmidt did the same and slid back the hood, locking it tight. That way there was no risk of being trapped in a burning wrecked plane.

'There!' de la Mazière cried out loud. Immediately to his front there was a straight stretch of bright white road, running along the crest of the hills, its one side formed by a fir forest, the other by some ploughed fields. It would have to do. Already angry blue sparks were beginning to explode from the radiator and the cockpit was filling with the sickening odour of escaping glycol fumes. De la Mazière flung back his helmet and sucked in a deep breath of clear air. He reduced throttle and lowered his flaps. Now he was down to a hundred metres, dragging a great black shadow behind him across the earth. A small group of dark figures ran out of what looked like a barn. He had no time to see whether they were civilians or soldiers. His concentration on that stretch of white road was total. Now it was looming ever larger. He was less than fifty metres above the ground.

He reduced speed even more. The Stuka started to vibrate wildly. The sweat poured down his face. He was handling the controls as if they were the most delicate instruments in the world. Twenty-five metres. He prayed his undercarriage was still intact. *Ten*!

He hit the road with a thunderclap. The Stuka reeled to the side at once. His undercarriage had been hit after all. There was the ear-searing rending sound of metal being shredded. The Stuka raced forward, trailing a huge wake of stone and dust behind it.

Violently de la Mazière was flung forward. The harness cut into his shoulders cruelly, ripping at the flesh, but it held. Something slapped into his right knee. He yelped with sheer agony. Suddenly there was a bend in the road. Beyond there was a low, tumbled-down house or farm. They were racing straight for it. Instinctively de la Mazière closed his eyes. Behind him Schmidt yelled something.

Abruptly they were flung into the air. For one agonizing second the two of them were suspended in space, clinging on desperately, as the Stuka stood on its nose, the road rearing up in front of them like a cobbled wall.

With a crash like thunder, it slammed down again. Right onto its belly, dust and wreckage shooting up on all sides, blinding the two occupants momentarily.

There was a loud echoing silence which seemed to go on for ever. A cold drop of sweat curled slowly down de la Mazière's blanched face. There was no sound save the drip-drip of escaping gasoline, still the two men were too dazed to move.

The drip-drip changed into a savage hiss. The gasoline was vaporizing against the white-hot metal of the shattered engine.

Smoke was beginning to seep through every chink in the wrecked plane. De la Mazière awoke to their danger. 'Schmidt,' he cried, tearing at his harness, 'get the hell out of here!' There was no reply.

He craned his head round.

Schmidt lay slumped against the cockpit, his face a mess of blood, two thick black trails of it seeping from his nostrils, but he was breathing all right. Perhaps he had just been knocked out by the impact of the crash.

Ignoring the pain in his knee, de la Mazière finished releasing himself. He crawled to Schmidt and grunting, pulled him out of the cockpit. He was a dead weight, but somehow or other he managed to drag him to the ground. There he slapped his face hard, noting with disgust how his palm was turned instantly red with the NCO's blood.

Schmidt's eyes flickered open weakly. Next to them the hiss of escaping gas was growing ever louder.

'What...' he groaned and closed his eyes again. De la Mazière hit him again — hard. 'Come on, man!' he cried savagely, 'we've got to get out of here. But I can't carry you far ... I've hurt my knee. Here, give me your arm.'

Somehow or other he managed to get Schmidt to his feet, supporting him under the shoulders. They started to hobble towards the firs to their left. The hiss turned into a sudden roar. De la Mazière felt the heat slap against the back of his torn flying suit. '*Los* ... *los!*' he urged frantically, 'the crate's going to go up any moment!'

The best they could, the two wounded men increased their pace. Would they make it? De la Mazière knew instinctively they wouldn't. He shoved Schmidt violently into the dry ditch at the side of the road. The NCO yelled. Next moment de la

Mazière dived in on top of him, face buried into the NCO's big back, hands clasped about his ears.

Not a moment too soon. The Stuka exploded with an ear-splitting roar. De la Mazière flung open his mouth to prevent his eardrums from bursting. The ground heaved and trembled like a trapped animal. A flood of burning gas swept down the road. Lying there, de la Mazière could feel the heat singe the small hairs at the back of his neck. Then the plane was burning fiercely, a tall black mushroom of smoke slowly ascending into the sky to mark their position for the enemy soldiers who would already be searching for them. 'Come on,' de la Mazière commanded, staggering to his feet and loosening the flap of his pistol holster, though he was exhausted and could have lain there for ever, 'let's make legs… They'll be coming soon.' Together the two of them staggered into the dark firs like men who were at the end of their tether.

Beyond the hills the smoke had begun to drift away. The noise of the firing had almost ceased now. A lone Stuka limped away below, obviously hit, hugging the hill ridge on the German side as it escaped.

Baron Karst, circling high above the battlefield, allowed himself a cold smile, though his icy-blue eyes did not light up. They had all tried — von Heiter, Furst Schwarz, young de la Mazière — and they had all failed. The bridge was still intact. If any one of them had hit it, they would have screamed out the news of their victory over the radio. He knew just how ambitious they all were. After all, they had joined the Armed SS, not out of conviction, a belief in the Holy Creed of National Socialism, as he had, but simply because the black guards had offered them quick promotion, a chance to re-establish their broken-down, impoverished families. His thin lips curled in contempt. In essence, they were all opportunists, his comrades, still believing in those old discredited values of the '*High aristocracy*'. At least his great-grandfather had been ennobled by the King of Prussia for his industry and ability on the shopfloor. The Karsts had not simply inherited a title; they had worked for it, just as he now worked to achieve the high honour which the Führer would undoubtedly bestow upon him if he succeeded.

Now he judged the time was just right. The French gunners, weaklings that they were, would soon be resting, thinking that they would not be attacked again for a while. This lull after the storm would be his opportunity to sneak in, take out the one battery which barred his approach to the bridge at Gmünd and then deal with the thing, once and for all. He opened up the throttle.

Hanneman noticed the change in speed immediately.

'You're going ahead with it, sir?' he asked politely enough, but there was steel in his voice.

'Of course,' Karst answered, feeling generous now.

'You know the dangers, sir?'

Karst did not answer. What was the peasant yokel yapping on about?

'You know the dangers to our own people, sir?' Hanneman persisted.

'Of course, of course,' Karst snapped, concentrating on his flying.

'And you persist?' this time Hanneman did not add the customary 'sir'.

'Yes, of course. War is war!' Karst cried in sudden anger. Why didn't the oaf shut up and concentrate on his task. He had been a fool to answer his damned impertinent questions from the start.

Now the hill-line that fringed the German bank of the River Sauer was coming into view. He swung a glance to the left. The French battery guarding the approach to the bridge from that side had to be somewhere there.

'Then, sir,' Hanneman said slowly and carefully, but doggedly, 'I will be forced to report you to the Squadron-Commander. Sir, you understand,' he added when Baron Karst did not reply.

'Naturally, I understand!' Karst rasped. 'Report all you like. But it will do you no good. What do the lives of a handful of peasants mean when the fate of the Reich is at stake?'

'But the peasants are the people!' Hanneman cried hotly.

'Be quiet, man!' Karst bellowed in sudden fury. 'I am now giving you a direct order to remain silent, Sergeant Hanneman! That is en —' He stopped short.

There was the flak battery, just above the straggle of houses running down the winding road through Gmünd which led to the bridge — and he had caught the French off guard, just as he had planned. Everywhere there were men pelting between the stacks of anti-aircraft shells towards their guns.

Karst's angry face broke into a cold deadly smile. 'Too late, too late!' he whispered, face almost wolfish now, as he went in for the kill.

Next moment the lone Stuka was hurtling down. The guns, the running Frenchmen, the straggle of black-roofed, white-painted cottages loomed up ever larger in his sights. He couldn't miss. Karst gritted his teeth, not taking his eyes off the scene below for one instant, fingers feeling instinctively for the bomb-release catch. He pressed it. The Stuka jerked. The bomb went whistling away and next instant he was sailing high into the sky, crying, 'Observe and report, damn you… Did we hit them?'

Hanneman craned his neck as the Stuka surged into the sky, the earth falling away behind them at a tremendous rate. He lost sight of the deadly black egg. He narrowed his eyes to slits trying to find it again.

And then. There was a tremendous roar above the village. A huge pillar of smoke, split by scarlet flashes, started to rush upwards immediately. It was followed by more and more, crackling their way down that narrow winding road towards the cottages like a Chinese firecracker. '*Report, damn you!*' Karst shrieked above the roar of the engine.

Hanneman closed his eyes momentarily, not wanting to see what was happening down there.

'REPORT!'

The first cottage erupted. Flame stabbed the smoke. Its roof blew off. Like a soft-boiled egg being hit too hard by a heavy spoon, its walls crumpled outwards and masonry was tumbling everywhere, as the shells exploding on both sides of the road ran on to the next humble cottage.

'*RE — PO — RT!*' Karst's savage cry thrust into his consciousness.

Hanneman swallowed hard as yet another cottage disintegrated and a thick pall of smoke started to descend mercifully over that terrible scene of destruction. 'I think you got the battery, sir,' he said miserably, 'and...' his voice broke ... 'the village of Gmünd too...'

The enemy were behind them. There was no mistaking those excited cries and calls in French. A sweat-lathered de la Mazière felt yet another branch lash his face, as they blundered onwards through the tight lines of firs, planted in rigid groves like soldiers standing on parade. He grasped his pistol in a damp hand, swearing that they wouldn't take him alive. Besides he knew it was no use surrendering. He was of the SS and he had been attempting to bomb their precious bridge all this long May day. They would stand him up against the nearest wall and shoot him out of hand like a dog. 'Come on, Schmidt,' he urged, trying to forget the agonizing pain which stabbed his knee like the sharp blade of a knife, 'keep going for God's sake!' He grabbed his companion's hand and they stumbled on.

They had been running east for half an hour now, ever since they had first spotted the line of cautious soldiers advancing across the fields with their rifles held at the port, like farmers braving heavy rain. For a while they had thought they had lost them in the thick fir forest, but now de la Mazière knew they had been mistaken. The French were determined to capture them — and from what he had seen so far there were too many of them for him and Schmidt to tackle with their Walthers.

Now the forest was beginning to thin out. Eyes wide and wild with excitement, his chest heaving crazily, his breath coming in harsh shallow gasps and sounding like air filtered through a cracked leathern bellows, de la Mazière could see fields beyond, a half or one kilometre away to the east. Suddenly they found themselves outside the firs. In front of them the ground ended abruptly. They were at the edge of some sort of a river, banked by an almost perpendicular cliff of slate. They staggered to a stop, shoulders drooping in defeat. The cries were getting louder again. Schmidt bent and rested his hands on his knees, his shoulders heaving violently as if he were sobbing, heart-broken.

De la Mazière stumbled a few more steps. The river was a hundred metres or so below. In their condition they would never be able to climb down the loose slate and gravel to it. But they had to! He saw the thorny bushes and stunted shrubs that ran down the cliff and remembered the Karl May stories of his youth. '*Los*, Schmidt,' he commanded, 'follow me and do the same as I do —' The first Frenchman emerged from the forest, shoulders heaving, as he brought up his long rifle.

De la Mazière snapped off a wild shot from the hip. The man screamed shrilly and slammed against the nearest tree, rifle tumbling from his suddenly nerveless fingers. He commenced sliding down its trunk, trailing blood after him. The others emerging behind him ducked back hastily into the cover of the forest.

De la Mazière lowered himself over the edge and taking his life into his hands let go. Immediately he began to fall. But not for long. Desperately he grabbed out. His mad progress was braked as his hands clutched and held one of the boughs — and it didn't break. He looked up at a gawping Schmidt, 'Come on, damn you … hurry up, man! It's the only way… Quick, let's get cracking before the frogs start coming out of the trees again.'

Not waiting to see whether or not Schmidt was following him, he let go again, fell a few metres and grabbed another branch, his arms ablaze with burning agony, feeling as if they were being snatched from their sockets.

Now they were halfway down the cliff, Schmidt following his example, urged on by the unreasoning overwhelming fear that if they weren't far enough down the cliff by the time the French ventured out of the firs again, they would be sitting ducks.

Now the river was only twenty or thirty metres away. They were going to do it. Gasping and retching the two fugitives fought their way downwards, their faces lashed cruelly by the branches, their knees and elbows skinned by the loose slate, fingers torn and bleeding.

'*Sales cons!*' a harsh angry voice cried from above.

De la Mazière didn't have to look up. He knew the French had left their hiding places. He waited for what was to come. There was the angry crackle of rifle fire. Tucking his head between his shoulders, like a man sheltering from driving rain, he let go again, as bullets began to whip up little spurts of stone all around him. A piece of flying slate sliced into his face. He yelped with pain and almost let go. Just in time he hung on. 'Look out, sir!' Schmidt gasped desperately.

De la Mazière threw an agonized look upwards. A dark round object was sailing down towards him. A grenade! He bent his head, hugging the slate as if it were a beloved woman. The grenade exploded some five metres away. He heard the shrapnel singing lethally through the air on all sides. The back of his head was buffeted by the blast. He gasped for breath and shouted, 'Schmidt ... let go... Drop into the river!'

Schmidt hesitated. 'I'm not a very good swimmer, sir!' he quavered.

'Well, now's the time to learn!' He ducked as another grenade came sailing through the air to explode against the side of the cliff, showering them with pieces of razor sharp flying slate. 'You first — then me. NOW ... *GO!*'

Schmidt closed his eyes and let go. He hit the river and disappeared in a huge spurt of flying white water. Next instant de la Mazière had let go too.

He gasped with shock. The water seemed freezing in his overheated condition. For a moment he panicked, unable to get his breath. 'Concentrate hard!' a harsh voice within his crazed head commanded, 'Don't think — just swim!'

Suddenly he found himself doing just that. Schmidt's head bobbed up next to him. 'Swim,' he gasped, tugging at his flying boots as he swam towards the NCO. 'And get your boots off if you can. They weigh a ton in this water.'

Somehow the two of them managed to do so, heading for the opposite bank, the wild angry French fire thrashing the water behind them purposelessly.

Five minutes later, they were stumbling through the thick muddy reeds on the other side, gasping like ancient asthmatics, bleeding from a dozen cuts and wounds, barefoot and cold, yet happy, unbelievably, ecstatically happy. 'A misspent youth,' de la Mazière choked, 'spent reading Karl May pays off sometimes, Schmidt, after all, don't it?'

Unable to speak, Sergeant 'Slack Arse' Schmidt nodded his enthusiastic agreement…

'The bridge!' Karst exclaimed.

A miserable Hanneman craned his neck. A thousand metres below there it lay, still intact, while all around in the valley lay the charred carcases of planes, crumpled wings, shattered fuselages, pathetic bits and pieces of aluminium set in circles of charred blackened grass. Everywhere, too, there were the great steaming bomb holes, surrounded by tiny still figures, sprawled out in the extravagant angles of the violently done to death.

Now the flak gunners on the Luxembourg side of the river were staggering exhausted back to their guns to meet this challenge, the loaders hugging heavy shells to feed their monsters, while the machine-gunners getting into action more quickly started blasting away. Tracer started to curve towards them in a dazzling parabola.

Baron Karst simply did not seem to notice. Now he was supremely confident, his approach to the bridge from the German bank unhindered by enemy fire. He had three 250 pound bombs left in his bomb bays. One of them was going to wreck that bridge. He tugged back the stick and the Stuka rose obediently for thirty seconds until he levelled out, directly above the bridge. Madly the gunners below fought their long-barrelled cannon round to fight him off. Karst's lean saturnine face broke into a contemptuous sneer. 'Too late … too late!' he hissed through gritted teeth. Next moment he jerked the stick forward and that old exhilarating race of death began once more.

Tracer raced up to meet him. It hissed to both sides of the furiously diving plane harmlessly. A first shell came screaming towards them like a mad comet, dragging a long fiery-red tail behind it. Instinctively Hanneman closed his eyes. It missed by a hundred metres. Karst's luck was still holding out.

Now the bridge seemed to fill the whole whirling crazy world below. Karst's fingers sought for the bomb release. It could be only a matter of seconds now. He tensed and commanded himself to breathe evenly. This time every procedure had to be carried out perfectly. He wouldn't get another chance. He *couldn't* miss! Behind him Hanneman prayed like he had never prayed since he had left his *Volksschule*. If the madman at the controls didn't pull out of the crazy dive soon, they'd crash. There was no doubt about that — they'd crash.

With a gasp, his loins heavy and strangely tumescent, Baron Karst pressed his bomb release. Once … twice … three times. For one long moment, he continued to dive, the Stuka's speed leaping madly now that the plane was freed of its heavy load, feasting his eyes on the bridge below, as if he could not get enough. Then he remembered his danger. He hit the brake. Next instant he jerked back the stick, tugging it to his heaving loins with both hands, the sweat pouring down his crimson face, eyes popping from his head.

A groaning thump. Another ... and another. Flame stabbed the sky. The Stuka rocked from side to side, as if punched by some gigantic hand. He almost lost the stick from his sweat-lathered hands. Madly he fought to regain control. As if suspended at the end of an enormous swing, the plane, buffeted by that tremendous blast, swung to and fro. Fierce hard gusts of wind shook and rattled it. The fuselage shrieked at every rivet. The engine howled furiously, as if the whole plane might disintegrate at any moment. The green needles of the instruments whirled and flickered crazily. The strain was almost unbearable.

Desperately Baron Karst, the veins bulging a bright purple at his temples, his ears exploding, the red mist threatening to overcome him at any moment, hung on.

Suddenly Hanneman was screaming in his ear. Wildly, hysterically, exultantly. '*OH, MY GOD!... YOU'VE HIT IT, SIR!... MY GOD, YOU'VE GONE AND HIT IT, SIR!... AT LAST...!*' He gave a great overwhelming sob, the tears streaming down his tortured lined face, gleaming with sweat, as if it had been rubbed with grease. '*IT'S... IT'S... ALL OVER, SIR...*'

In that very same instant, Karst regained control. Something exploded within him. He screamed as if in the throes of sexual passion. As the Stuka soared upwards with an exhilarating leap, his lower body was racked with an almost unbearable ecstasy. Next instant his loins were flooded joyously. He had done it! He had destroyed the bridge at Gmünd...

CHAPTER 7

Dawn came reluctantly. The sun poised hesitantly on the horizon to the east, as if not daring to rise any further and illuminate this stark, war-torn landscape of horror.

The two of them swayed to a halt, footsore and unutterably weary, staggering like drunks, saying nothing, simply viewing that awesome, brooding scene.

Now they knew they were safe. There was no more danger. They were back in the Reich. The Frenchmen who had survived on the eastern bank had fled, wading through the Sauer like they had just done, hurrying back to Luxembourg.

Indeed the French were pulling out altogether. Now the bridge at Gmünd had been destroyed and Rommel was pushing hard on the other side of the River Meuse, there was no future for the French Army in Luxembourg, or Belgium either, for that matter. Soon they would begin their great retreat to commence the defence of their own country against the armoured juggernaut about to descend upon them.

But the two tattered men, still bleeding from a dozen wounds, were uninterested in the victory at Gmünd and what would follow it soon. They simply stood and stared as the first ugly-white light of the new dawn revealed the tragedy at Gmünd in all its harsh brutality.

The bombers had done their work well. The great oaks which had once lined the twisting curving road to the river were now gaunt outsized toothpicks. Every cottage had been hit and shattered. Jagged chunks of stonework lay everywhere, blocking the road, smoke drifting lazily here and there from a charred beam, grotesquely twisted pieces of iron work protruding from the heaps of rubble. Everywhere there was discarded equipment mixed up with the pathetic bits and pieces of the villagers — steel helmets, smashed rifles, discarded gas masks heaped in confusion with broken water-pitchers, bent, twisted pans, splintered chairs.

But it wasn't the shattered cottages which held the two sleepwalkers' attention. It was the dead. They were heaped everywhere, men, women and children. A woman of about thirty, completely naked, lying face downwards in the gutter; two little boys clinging tightly to one another, faces buried in the rubble, legs raised in the air stiffly; a fat old man sitting on a chair, his enormous belly split open, the viscera swelling out of the hole like a giant violet sea-anemone; a crisp charred dwarf of a man reduced to half his size by the tremendous heat; a baby apparently sleeping innocently in an undamaged perambulator, bedded in the thick red jelly of its own blood; a head, complete with green peaked cap, lying as if tossed carelessly away, in the gutter; a naked hand poked out of the rubble, fingers outstretched, as if pleading with heaven for mercy; a dead soldier, his genitals popped out of his flies like ghastly waxen fruit. On all sides there were horrors, horrors, horrors...

'They ... they're all German, sir,' Schmidt said in a tiny awed voice, 'same as us ... and we killed them...' His voice trailed away and two lone tears began to course slowly down his ashen, dirty face.

'The price of victory,' de la Mazière said without conviction trying, but failing to take his gaze from a dead girl with blonde plaits and a flowered peasant dress whose eyes stared up at him unwinkingly from her waxen face, as if in accusation. 'The price of victory...' He felt unutterably tired and dejected. Their victory at Gmünd had turned to bitter ashes in his mouth.

Nothing, he knew with the instant overwhelming clarity of a sudden vision, would ever be the same again for him. Already he could see the flames spreading from one sky to another.

From Germany to the flatlands of Belgium and France; from thence to the teeming cities of England... On and on, destroying, consuming, wrecking all before them, sweeping all before them in a terrible firestorm, until finally they had set the whole world aflame.

Silently he turned, unable to face that naked unwinking girls gaze any longer. He could not clamber over the corpses to reach the top of the hill. Their eyes would be watching him all the while. He began to move along the river bank. Wordlessly Sergeant Schmidt did the same and trailed after him, his big shoulders bent, as if in complete abject defeat...

BOOK 3: *TO GAIN A FORTUNE*

CHAPTER 1

An ominous silence prevailed. There was no sound save for the lazy hum of the bees and far, far away a strange, mechanical rumbling. Up above, the burning blue June sky was empty. There was not a plane in sight. A faint wind blew the warm sea air across the ripening fields of French corn. It was an idyllic scene. The war seemed light-years away.

But it wasn't. The sandy-haired soldiers, collarless shirts black with sweat, balmorals thrust to the backs of their shaven skulls, to protect them from the burning sun, were ready for the kill. All morning the products of Glasgow's slums had been waiting, labouring mightily since dawn, preparing their positions for what was soon to come. The glittering white coastal road, running dead straight along the high cliffs for ten kilometres, was barred by a confused mess of looted French farm carts, hay wagons and barrels of concrete. Mines had been strung across the road and to both sides of it, barbed wire, three lines of it, had been implanted.

Sandbags had been heaped around the cellar windows of the pre-war boarding houses, gun pits had been dug, and up high in the grey Gothic steeple, an observer watched and waited, ready to give the signal in an instant to the men dug in everywhere; while out in the bay, the lean grey shape of a British destroyer cut the flat green sea, guns already trained on the road along which they *had* to come. The Black Watch, known in the Old War as 'the Ladies from Hell', were ready to do battle with the approaching Germans once again.

For three weeks the whole of the British Expeditionary Force had been retreating across Belgium and Northern France, fighting and retreating, pursued by the panzers and the murderous dive-bombers which had flung themselves out of the sky in suicidal attacks every time the soldiers had attempted to dig in and forced them yet once again to join that weary, disheartened stream flowing towards the Channel Ports and the unknown.

Now there was little further to go. To their rear lay only the Channel and beyond that England itself. The time for running had come to an end at last. So far and no more.

Now the motto was — *stand, fight, win or die!* And the undersized, bandy-legged Jocks baking out there in the dry rustling cornfields on both sides of the glaring, white coastal road knew it. This time they would beat the Hun — or die in the damned attempt.

The Germans would not get within artillery distance of the port of St Valery, to which the divisional staff had retreated. The C.O. had promised the divisional commander General Fortune personally that now the line would hold. The honour of the Black Watch was at stake. This time the 'Ladies from Hell' would save the guid old 51st Highland Division as it had done many times before in 1914-1918.

The minutes ticked by leadenly. There was little movement to their front, though high up in the steeple the watching observer noted automatically the red flare far away that sailed into the gleaming blue sky to fall moments later like a dying angel. It was the signal. He whirled his field telephone and spoke in a subdued whisper to the anxious-faced officers grouped below in the cobbled square. Hurriedly the runners, packs bouncing up and down on their skinny backs, doubled off to the companies to carry the new warning.

More time passed. Out at sea the destroyer began to lower its 4.5-inch guns. Tiny figures ran up and down the length of the deck lugging ammunition. Men in overalls started to spray the superstructure with sea-water from the hosepipes in case of fire. On the bridge was the glint of binoculars in the blinding sun as the officers directed their attention on the coastal road, the way the tanks would come.

Suddenly, quite surprisingly, there they were. A slow thoughtful line of men in grey, well spread out, weapons held at the port, working their way through the corn carefully, methodically, parting the dry, waist-high rasping stalks, as if they were looking for something hidden there.

There was the metallic click of rifle bolts being drawn back. Men squirmed as they tried to find a more comfortable position in the parched holes. Balmorals were pushed down deep over foreheads to keep out the glare of the slanting sunrays. Here and there, some leathern-faced, wizened veteran of the North-West Frontier carefully licked his thumb and applied the saliva to his foresight. The metallic rattle and rusty squeak of tank tracks grew louder. Back in the square, the Black Watch's C.O. said something hastily into his radio transmitter, attached to the back of the crouched sweating signaller, his voice low, as if the approaching enemy might well hear him.

Birds flew up from the corn, disturbed by the men in grey. A rabbit shot out of the fields and ran across the road, unaware that eight hundred armed men were watching him. In the great poplars that lined the road, the rooks crowed in hoarse approval. The men in grey, so slow, so careful, so systematic, came ever closer to the marker sticks cunningly planted that very morning in the corn to record their progress, unwittingly marching towards their death. Here and there a parched-lip

Jock counted off the yards, as they did so. '*Six hundred … five fifty … five hundred yards … four … three hundred and fifty…*'

'*SCOTLAND FOR EVER!*' the great hoarse roar erupted suddenly all along the hidden line. '*HELL'S LAST ISSUE — HERE WE ARE!*'

It was the signal.

A heavy machine gun burst into life. Sweeping from left to right the tracer raced across the tops of the corn and slammed into the first rank of Germans. They went down, suddenly galvanized into violent frenetic action, arms and legs flailing, screaming thinly as their bodies were ripped apart.

Now more Germans came into sight, line after line of them, no longer so slow now, their officers and NCOs yelling angry exhortations, whistles shrilling urgently.

The whole front of the Black Watch erupted in flame. Machine guns rattled, rifles cracked, mortars belched obscenely. Still the Germans advanced, toylike, trivial, ineffective against the metal wrath of the machine guns and mortars. Bravely the German panzer grenadiers of General Rommel's Seventh Armoured Division advanced to their death, whole lines of them withering away in that terrible fire until the cornfield was full of their still grey corpses.

Now, however, their iron discipline was beginning to break at last. Above the screams of agony, the cries, the angry bellows, the slow chatter of the Scots' machine guns sounding like angry hoarse woodpeckers, there was the new high-pitched hysterical screech of German machine-guns. They were going to ground, perhaps while others of the panzer grenadiers attempted to turn the Black Watch's flank.

To no avail! The little men from the slums of the Gorbals were waiting for them there, hidden in the barns and dug in deep in the sandbagged cellars. The Germans didn't stand a chance. They went down on all sides, and the Jocks working their bolts back and forth like clockwork could hear the satisfying thwack-thwack of their slugs slapping into the big Germans as they rushed screaming into the disastrous attack. Not one of them got closer to the Jocks' positions than a hundred metres.

Scarlet flame stabbed the smoke. Screaming obscenely, mad with both fear and anger, the little men mowed the
Germans down, showing no mercy, carried away with the terrible awesome blood-lust of battle, screaming their battle cry over and over again, '*Scotland for Ever!*' as they fired, fired, fired…

For a little while longer the grenadiers came on. For one more minute they were running, living, shouting men. The next they were dead or dying, writhing in their mortal agony in the corn, staining it red with their blood, thrashing it with their agonized limbs, gasping out the last of their short young lives, faces ashen and contorted with the unbelievable, unbearable pain. Then the survivors were streaming to the rear, blundering blindly through the corn, pushing and jostling each other in their panic, throwing away their weapons in their overwhelming, unreasoning fear; and the Jocks' officers were shrilling on their whistles, crying, '*Cease fire, will you … cease fire, damn your eye s… They've gone!*'

As the last shots petered away, there was a hellish whine, an obscene howl, and the first shells of the German mortar barrage came screaming through the blazing summer sky. The first German attack on the positions of the 51st Highland Division around St Valery had failed miserably. But as the Jocks cowered, faces still triumphant, in their cellars and slit trenches, feeling the very earth quiver and quake beneath them under that tremendous bombardment, they knew the Huns would be back, that they would — and they would be waiting for them…

The dawn silence was broken by a squeaking, an ominous rumbling, a series of throaty metallic coughs like the awakening groans of some fearsome primeval monster, rousing itself for the ruthless slaughter of the new day.

'Stand to, there!' the harsh voices of the NCOs ran down the Black Watch's line. 'Hands off yer cocks … and on with yer socks!'… 'They're coming!'

Those of the little men who had been able to sleep during the night-long barrage and the sudden echoing silence which had followed, popped their dirty unshaven faces above the parapets of their trenches and stared hard to the north. Here and there a man gasped in horror. The Catholics among them crossed themselves solemnly. An officer said in an awed whisper, 'Oh, my fucking God, the whole of the German Army!'

A solid column was advancing upon them ponderously. Rumbling through the corn, came an armoured battering ram, tanks to the front, armoured cars to each flank, within the centre, truck after truck crowded with infantry. Steadily the German column came closer: a great black stark juggernaut of awesome menace, the metal hides of the monsters in front slowly being tinged a blood-red in the first rays of the ascending sun.

Now the tensed, awed Jocks could see the cannon of the tanks in the lead begin to swing to left and right like the snouts of primeval monsters scenting out their prey. They sank deeper and deeper into their pits. What could they do against such monsters with their puny weapons?

With startling suddenness, the divisional artillery somewhere to the rear crashed into action. Cherry-red spurts of flame cut the dawn greyness to their rear. Twenty-five-pounder shells screamed exultantly over the helmeted heads of the Jocks to plunge down on the advancing columns. Out at sea the Aldis lamps began to flicker their white urgent messages. The destroyer was coming in again to support them. Great brown steaming holes began to appear everywhere in the fields to the Jocks' front. Here and there one of the monsters reeled to a halt, its long overhanging gun sinking as if it had been mortally stricken.

Still the rest crawled on with no break in their tempo, while the Jocks crouched in their pits, their ears deafened by the thunder of the guns and the might of those massed engines, letting the full and terrible fascination of that evil crawling, blood-red mass sink into their dazed minds for ever.

Now the leading monsters split into two columns, while the others remained to protect the truck-borne infantry. Twin streams of black-painted monsters, their armour glowing in that blood-red dawn, as if it were on fire, waddled to left and right. Like giant ants on the march, unseeing, unfeeling, unable to be deflected from their grim purpose — not even the exploding shells which showered them with stones and dirt and made them shake violently, as if hit by a sudden great wind, seemed to be able to stop them — they began to encircle the Black Watch's positions.

Suddenly brazen lights flashed out to sea. The air was torn apart by a tremendous howl — like a giant piece of canvas being ripped. A circle of blinding, white, glowing incandescent flame engulfed the leading tanks. Huge spurts of flame shot high into the sky. Mark IV tanks rocked violently everywhere and disappeared into the whirling mass of debris and the flying clouds of thick black oily smoke.

In an instant the two columns had come to a halt. Vehicles were sprawled, suddenly shattered and burning everywhere, tracks rolled out behind them like broken limbs, great gleaming silver holes skewered into the turrets and hulls.

Again the destroyer's guns spoke. There was a thunder, a rush, a terrifying whoosh — and again tanks reeled under the hammer-blows. Now white-faced, shocked tankmen were staggering from their shattered, crippled vehicles, some already beating at the greedy flames creeping up their overalls, others too dazed to do anything but stand and sway there until the Jocks' merciless bullets cut them down into the burning corn.

Now the Jocks were swarming out of their trenches, their officers unable to hold them, carried away by that savage aggressive fury of their Celtic ancestors. A group went down under a tank's tracks, its driver whirling round and round, pulping and churning the Scots' bodies into a blood-red gore before rumbling on, a lone arm hanging from the suddenly crimson tracks, jolted back and forth for a fleeting second, as if waving goodbye to the cardboard like squashed figures of its dead comrades.

But the crazed rush of the Black Watch was not be stopped. Everywhere they were coming out of the hedges and ditches, popping up out of the corn, tackling the stalled monsters like a myriad bandy-legged Davids. Dark figures set a stark black against the blood-red ball of the sun, they raced for the tanks. Sticky grenades clanged hollowly against the monsters' metal sides. A long moment of fear as long as eternity itself. A great hollow boom and the inside of the Mark IV would be a whirling frantic maelstrom of flying steel, cutting down everything in its path, turning the interior into a charnel house of severed limbs, a bath of blood-red steaming gore.

Desperately the panicked tank crews tried to fight back. Machine guns chattered. Everywhere the running Jocks went down, spines curved grotesquely in that final burning agony, as their clawed hands flung upwards to the unfeeling heavens as if pleading for mercy.

But they couldn't kill them all and the battle-crazed Jocks were everywhere, screaming, stabbing, slaughtering. On all sides tanks lay blazing and crippled while their crews, those who had survived, sprawled on the ground supinely like dumb animals accepting their inevitable fate, and the little men slashed and stabbed at them with their entrenching tools, bayonets, boots, anything, until their faces were a bloody, unrecognisable welter of red gore and smashed, gleaming white bone.

It was too much for the rest. Whistles began to shrill. Red flares sailed into the sky urgently. Mortar fire started to descend upon the Jocks, ragged and uncertain. Slowly the column began to withdraw before this terrible Celtic fury. In their panic, drivers smashed into each other. A truck attempting to turn ran into a poplar on the side of the road, spilling its infantry onto the cobbles where they were crushed to death by the whirling tracks of one of their own tanks. Another tank ran off the same road and lay there on its back, tracks flailing helplessly, like a great black beetle.

Suddenly it was no longer a withdrawal, but a retreat. For the first time in the month-old campaign, General Erwin Rommel's vaunted Seventh Panzer Division, the Victor of the Battle of the Meuse, was running away!

CHAPTER 2

General Rommel peered through the telescope at the port some two kilometres away. Here and there a column of smoke rose slowly to the sky, as if the Tommies might well be burning papers and equipment. But there were others everywhere, lugging sandbags, unrolling concertinas of barbed wire, stripped to the waist in the hot morning sun, digging ditches. He sniffed. It didn't look to him as if the men down there at St Valery were preparing to surrender — just yet. Despite the fact that the French port was cut off from the land, General Fortune, his opposite number, and his 51st Highland Division, seemed to be readying themselves for an all-out defence.

Rommel lowered the telescope and stroked his heavy chin thoughtfully. All around him his staff officers waited, wondering what his decision would be. They knew just how ambitious their commander was. He still had Hitler's ear. But what might happen if the British beat him at St Valery, or managed to snatch away the trapped Division by sea, as they had done only a few days ago at Dunkirk? The Führer, they all knew, was a fickle man, given to moods and whims. He could dismiss Rommel, his current favourite, as easily as clicking his fingers. Rommel desperately needed a last victory before the British were run out of Europe for good. It might well mean the difference between being fired from his command and the command of a new corps, the Swabian General's undoubted aim.

Rommel turned on them, his broad face glazed with sweat in the hot sun as theirs were, too. 'Gentlemen, I have made my decision. I think that the Tommies will make a fight for it. It is clear to me that this General Fortune of theirs,' he smiled suddenly, but the eyes remained cold. 'What an unfortunate name, for I shall ensure that he has no fortune, eh?'

His staff officers smiled politely and waited, wishing their commander would get on with it and they could go. The flies were beginning to become troublesome, here on the wooded height overlooking St Valery.

'Well, as I was saying, it is clear to me that this Fortune fellow is going to make a stand. He has no problems to sea, for the Royal Navy will ensure he is protected there. So he will undoubtedly place the bulk of his force in a defensive semi-circle around the port, covering the coastal road and the low heights to the east, that is, in the centre of his perimeter.' He smiled again. 'Fortune is a conventional general and he will plan a conventional defensive perimeter.'

His officers nodded their agreement. Even now after four weeks of battle, the British commanders had not become accustomed to the new tactics of the *blitzkrieg*. They still fought as if this was 1914-1918 and they were fighting a positional kind of war in the trenches.

'General Rommel, however,' their commander continued with a cynical glance around their faces, 'is *not* a conventional commander. He does not fight a war according to the rules of one of those celebrated English tea-parties of theirs. Once this morning's drive has broken through the coastal road so that we can bring up the Corps' heavy artillery and have a go at that damned destroyer that Fortune has got out there in the bay, I shall —' He stopped short, his eyes suddenly full of total, absolute disbelief.

Bewildered, his staff officers followed the direction of the General's gaze.

Down below figures in field-grey were beginning to stream by and already they could hear them cursing, weeping, yelling at each other. Some wore bloody bandages, others held shattered limbs, holding them up piteously at regular intervals as if the sight explained everything. Many were without tunics or helmets. A few lacked weapons.

A fat bareheaded Major appeared from nowhere. He tried to stop these strange men, bellowing with rage, grabbing bewildered zombie-like soldiers and forcing them to halt. But they swept by him. He drew his revolver, then slowly and sadly he replaced it and walked away, shoulders heaving as if he were sobbing.

'*Himmel, Herr Gott!*' Rommel cursed, 'Follow me, gentlemen. At once!'

Abruptly the heavy-set, middle-aged staff officers found themselves running behind their commander down the hill towards the strangers.

Rommel, his face a mask of crimson anger, came to a stumbling halt.

A helmetless soldier with the silver stars of a lieutenant on his shoulders lurched towards him, dragging a rifle behind him by its sling. He looked unutterably weary, his face beet-red with a trickle of blackened, caked blood down the left cheek, his tongue hanging out of the side of his mouth. He looked like a man who had somehow survived a hanging.

Rommel slapped his hand to his pistol holster. '*Leutnant*,' he rasped, 'come here — at once!'

'Kiss my arse,' the soldier gasped.

The staff officers started, as if they had just been punched in the stomach.

Rommel's eyes blazed. He reached out and grabbing the lieutenant by the front of his blood-stained sweat-blackened shirt, pulled him towards him; he reached for his pistol. Face contorted with rage, he pulled it out and placed the muzzle just below the officer's chin. 'Listen to me, you wretch,' he choked through gritted teeth, 'I shall blow your miserable head off in one minute flat. What happened, man? Out with it, now!'

Stuttering, gulping, eyes rolling wildly, as if he might collapse or begin to scream at any moment, the young officer told the Commanding General what had happened out on the coastal road when his regiment had attempted to overrun the positions of the British infantry. 'My company was destroyed, sir,' he ended with a gulp. 'Gone, vanished, disappeared. We didn't —'

Deliberately, knowing he had to shut the broken man up immediately, for there was the sound of marching feet behind him which indicated that new troops were coming up, he swung back his hand and slapped the officer hard across the face. He staggered back, tears streaming down his cheeks. 'Now,' Rommel barked harshly, 'report to the provost marshal immediately. Tell him to place you under close arrest. You will be court-martialled in due course.' He dismissed the sobbing man and turned to the nearest staff officer, 'Kurt.'

'Sir?'

'Form a stop line immediately. Use my headquarters guard company if you wish, anybody, cooks and clerks — and stop this rabble at once,' he indicated the stream of weary beaten men lurching by. 'I don't want real fighting men to see them. Bed them down, feed them, arm them and send them back to the line tomorrow. Now get on with it.' Without pausing for breath once, Rommel issued a stream of orders to meet the new situation occasioned by his defeat on the coast. Outwardly his stern face showed no emotion and he seemed in full control of himself. Inwardly he fumed, his mind racing to meet the new situation, a malicious little voice constantly reminding him of the effect this defeat might have at the *High Command*. There were plenty of generals there who hated him and thought of him as an opportunist who had somehow gained the Führer's ear. They would be only too glad to see him fall from grace.

His face hardened. For nearly thirty years now he had been a soldier, working his way with infinite slowness up the ladder of promotion. My God, how he had prayed all those long years of garrison duty in those dusty provincial towns in the backwaters of the Reich, waiting for the

next step in his career! Now he had his war, something desired fervently by all professional soldiers; for it was war that ensured rapid promotions. He was already pushing fifty. If he ever wanted to gain the high rank he coveted, it was now or never. By the time this summer was out, the Tommies would be finished — they had no staying power, he knew that — and the war would be over. After all, his pension *was* important!

He finished his orders to meet the new situation and turned to his new aide, dark eyes angry and blazing. 'Jesus, Maria, Joseph,' he cried fervently, fists clenched into white-knuckled balls against outrageous fate, 'Where are my Stukas, Heinz?... Where is my aerial artillery now that I need it so desperately...? Where is my First SS Stuka Squadron?'

General Rommel flung a despairing look at the burning blue heavens, devoid of that gull-winged silhouette which meant hope and success, '*WHERE?*'...

CHAPTER 3

'*Willya cast yer glassy orbs on that ass!*' Sergeant Hanneman breathed in awe. '*All that meat!*'

Next to him Slack Arse Schmidt, his running-mate, who still wore carpet slippers from his long ordeal with de la Mazière, crossed himself reverently, as the half-naked whore disappeared above them on the landing, taking with her her beautiful bare arse. The brothel next to the station at Reims was packed with excited, sex-starved soldiers, shuffling forward impatiently to where the fat, black-clad madam with her peroxided hair presided over her ringing cash-register, while above the bedsprings squeaked mightily.

Hanneman pushed by a line of infantrymen, clad in full combat gear, including rifles and helmets, and dug his awed running-mate in the ribs. 'Hark to those bed springs, Slack Arse,' he said gleefully, ignoring the angry murmurs on all sides in that smoke-filled crowded room, 'Ain't that beautiful music? Better 'n all Beethoven's symphonies put together — and then some.' He pushed his fatigue cap to the back of his cropped head. 'By the Great Whore of Buxtehude, am I going to dance a mattress polka this afternoon!' He licked his lips in anticipation and yanking the bottle of beer out of the hand of one of the waiting infantrymen took a great pull, handing it back to him virtually empty, with a polite belch. 'Could have been colder, stubblehopper,' he commented, and passed on leaving the infantryman speechless.

Flanked by Slack Arse, Hanneman faced the blonde madam, whose massive white breasts seemed about to explode out of her tight black silk bodice. '*Bon jour,*' he began, beaming winningly at her. 'Me want two,' he held up two fingers like small sausages to indicate his need. '*Compris*, two!' he fumbled in his pigeon French for the word he needed, and failed. He filled the gap with an obscene gesture of his right thumb and two fingers.

The madam looked at him coldly, 'I'll have none of that kind of piggery in my establishment,' she said in throaty, but perfect German. 'I don't cater for that kind of *schweinerei*, compris?'

Hanneman's mouth fell open. 'Did you hear that, Slack Arse, the frog can speak our lingo nearly as good as what I can —'

Hanneman stopped short. A heavy gnarled hand descended heavily on his shoulder and his nostrils were suddenly assailed by the stink of sweat, stale tobacco smoke and schnapps. He turned round. An angry brick-red face stared back at him above a heavy body dressed in the uniform of the German infantry, muscled brutally around the shoulders.

Hanneman smiled winningly. '*Ist was, Kamerad?*' he asked mildly. The big infantryman thrust a fist like a small steam-shovel under Hanneman's nose. 'Wait yer turn, *flyboy*!' he growled in a thick Berlin accent. 'Get back in line if you know what's good for yer, *flyboy*!' There was a murmur of agreement from the waiting infantrymen. 'But we're in a hurry,' Hanneman said, as if that were explanation enough. 'We've got to be back at the Field in an hour, comrade.'

'We've got to be back at the Field in an hour, comrade!' the infantryman mimicked in a high falsetto, doing a few tripping steps, swaying his huge buttocks in an affected manner, his little fingers extended. Then his voice became gruff and menacing again. 'And *we've* got to be at the front this night, *comrade!*'

Hanneman pointed to the newly won Iron Cross, First Class, on his broad chest, still smiling hugely.

The infantryman wasn't impressed. 'Probably won it for having the cleanest aeroplane or something,' he cried and his listeners laughed uproariously. 'And look at the other fart — he's even wearing slippers. Probably got nice little room back at the field with his Goethe poems and herbal tea where he can put his feet up.'

At the cash register the blonde madam laughed so much at this witty sally that one of her massive breasts popped out of the black silk cage. It was a minute before she realized that it had done so, but when she saw the hungry looks suddenly appearing in the infantrymen's eyes, she stuffed it back hurriedly, saying loudly, 'Yer don't need to look. There's nothing for free here, you young pigs!'

Slack Arse Schmidt, his face an angry red, looked at the giant infantryman. 'Did you say something about me, or was yer just firing yer fart cannon?'

The infantrymen howled.

'Shove it, aspagarus Tarzan!' the big one growled, keeping his small piglike eyes fixed on Hanneman, who was still smiling, as if his mouth was fixed in that position for all eternity.

'Did I hear right?' Slack Arse said through gritted teeth, right hand suddenly buried deep in his pocket.

'Of course yer did, you poison dwarf, or have yer been eating big beans?' He beamed at his comrades proudly.

'You realize, comrade,' Hanneman said in tones of sweet reason, 'that you *are* addressing two senior NCOs of the Great German Air Force, don't you?'

'Flyboys,' the infantryman howled, 'I've shat 'em!' He raised his right leg as if to emphasize his point, and ripped off a great dry fart that sent the surprised madam staggering back against the wall, her powdered face pale with shock.

It was then that Slack Arse Schmidt's fist flashed from his pocket. Filled with five-franc pieces, it slammed into the hulking infantryman's jaw with the impact of a sledgehammer. He went reeling back, spitting out teeth, suddenly cross-eyed, to smash into the madam. She fell on her back, skirt riding up to reveal an ample expanse of fat white flesh — and the fact that she was not wearing knickers on account of the June heat.

In an instant all was confusion, pandemonium. Men were swapping punches on all sides. A mirror shattered. An infantryman, complete with pack and rifle, flew through the window. Whistles shrilled outside urgently. From above half-naked women poured down the stairs, accompanied by men trying to pull on their boots and tunics. A man was screaming in sheer agony, 'But I've got my foreskin caught in the springs, mates!' From outside came the roar of engines, the squeal of brakes and angry, official shouts.

Carefully crawling through the shattered glass, the unconscious bodies, while above him men slugged it out with relentless fury and the military police hammered at the door of the whorehouse with their rifle butts, Hanneman took a last look at the stupefied madam, still lying there with her black skirt up about her waist. He shook his head in mock sadness. 'What a waste of lovely grub, Slack Arse. Just look at them pearly gates, willya… Ah, well, come on, comrade, let's get out of here before the Chaindogs nab us.' Mumbling something about 'man's inhumanity to man,' he crawled on towards the back door.

The First SS Stuka Squadron's last day in Reims had begun badly…

'I say, de la Mazière, can I enter, bearing a small cloud?' Hanno von Heiter called from behind the door of the mess.

De la Mazière looked up from the new copy of *Signal* and chuckled. Hanno had his cap at the back of his head and his handsome young face was flushed. He was obviously nearly drunk again, but then ever since the attack on the bridge at Gmünd with its disastrous losses, he had been drunk most of the time. 'Of course, old horse, enter, bearing your cloud with you.' He stopped short, seeing the long chain that the young officer trailed behind him. 'But what's *that* in hell's name?'

Hanno von Heiter's gaze fell to his highly polished riding boots, as if he were somehow ashamed.

De la Mazière's smile deepened and he tossed the Army magazine onto the nearest chair. Hanno really was a card. Ever since their new senior flight commander Baron Karst, now the proud possessor of the Knight's Cross of the Iron Cross for his exploits at the bridge, had taken von Heiter to task on account of his drinking, the latter wandered in and out of the mess talking drunkenly of the 'cloud over my head'. 'Holy strawsack, Hanno, don't be shy! Drag in your cloud and take the weight off your feet.'

Hanno tugged at the long chain and nearly fell through the door, dragging behind him what appeared to be a woolly sausage on four legs, the front and end of the sausage tied up with pink ribbons.

'Oh my God,' de la Mazière groaned, eyes wide with amazement, 'not a shitting poodle, Hanno! *Not that!*'

Hanno looked down at the absurd dog with its spindly legs and trimmed floppy ears, which had cocked its leg against the nearest armchair and was beginning to urinate there lazily, as it started to stake out its territory.

'A feller's got to have a mascot, de la Mazière,' Hanno von Heiter said miserably and sank down in the chair next to de la Mazière, who was holding back his laughter with the greatest of difficulty. 'I know, I know what everybody will say — an SS officer parading around with that. I'm some kind of warm brother. But it's the only damned thing the local pet shop had. Fiffi, it's called,' he added a little hopelessly, as the dog proceeded to the next armchair and began to repeat its performance. 'Good dog, Fiffi, but don't do that … *please!*'

The dog gave him a haughty glance out of the side of its black eyes, and trotted on with its spindly legs to the next chair.

'But why, Hanno?' de la Mazière found his voice at last.

Outside a dispatch rider roared by in one hell of a hurry. Idly de la Mazière wondered why. The Squadron had been stood down ever since the slaughter of the Stukas at the bridge. Officially the explanation of their inactivity, when the armoured divisions were screaming out for every single Stuka they could lay their hands on in the great drive west, was that the First SS Stuka Squadron needed time to replace losses and absorb new pilots. Within the Squadron, however, it was an open secret that Göring had placed an unofficial ban on their flying any more. There were going to be no more banner headlines such as the ones that had followed the destruction of the bridge at Gmünd as long as *he* was the head of the German Air Force.

Hanno von Heiter looked at his friend, his young face no longer flushed, his eyes steady. 'Without a mascot, de la Mazière, I've had it. I know *you* might think such things rot. But I don't. Without a mascot, I think…' He stopped short.

Outside the dispatch rider had raced to a stop in a huge cloud of white dust outside the Squadron Office. De la

Mazière frowned. Where's the fire? he asked himself, as the leather-clad, begoggled rider pushed inside the shack.

'I was with young von Degenhardt this morning,' Hanno von Heiter broke his silence. 'At the hospital, you know.'

De la Mazière's smile vanished. He nodded. Von Degenhardt had pressed home his attack on the bridge with reckless courage, and had been shot down in a ball of flame. When he had been reached, there had been little of his face left and his hands were simply red stumps. Now he lay in a kind of white helmet of plaster of Paris. He could not speak, see or swallow, being fed by a tube inserted in the mask down to his stomach. 'How is he, Hanno?' de la Mazière asked gently.

'Dying. The C.O's with him now.' There was a look of pleading almost in Hanno von Heiter's young face. 'After I saw him this morning, I went to the nearest French pet shop and bought Fiffi.' He swallowed hard. 'I *had* to! That couldn't happen to me, de la Mazière. I had to have a mascot, de la Mazière. *Do you understand?*' he gripped the other officer's hand until it hurt, his shoulders bent and heaving. Gently de la Mazière patted him on the shoulder, glad that they were alone in the mess. He couldn't have stood Baron Karst's supercilious sneers at this moment, 'I understand, Hanno,' he whispered, thinking of that dead girl in her blood-stained dress and her accusing eyes, 'I understand, well…'

Lieutenant-Colonel Greim stood up as the nurse came in. She was old, ugly and very fat, but gentle. Apparently she was the only one in the whole Field Hospital who had the nerves to deal with von Degenhardt. She smiled slightly and waddled to the thing on the bed, the pouring-beaker held in her pudgy hand. Bending breathlessly, for she was really gross, she put her lips to the window cut in the plaster mask near von Degenhardt's ear so that he could understand when they were going to do something to him. 'Some soup for you, Lieutenant,' she said softly. 'Nice pea soup. I cooked it for you myself. Now promise you'll drink it all up. It'll make you fit and well.' She straightened up with a sigh and reached for the funnel on the metal table at the side of the cot.

Greim frowned. Normally the poor young swine gave some sort of signal — a wave of the hand or something — when they were about to feed him through the tube. This time there was nothing.

The gross sister noticed too. She put down the funnel again and tapped the hard cast above where von Degenhardt's skull would be. 'Soup,' she said again sweetly.

Again there was no answering sign.

She frowned and tapped once more.

Still there was no answer.

A cold chill ran down Greim's spine.

The sister stared carefully at the lower tube through which von Degenhardt breathed. It did not move and there was not the usual soft flutter-and-hiss. His breathing had stopped. Slowly she put down the bowl of soup and turned to Lieutenant-Colonel Greim, two large tears trickling lazily down her gross old face. She nodded.

He was dead.

Blind, deaf, wordless, von Degenhardt, trapped in his white plaster dome, had died the loneliest death of all. Slowly the weeping sister began to draw the sheet over the white dome.

Dazed a little, blinking a little in the sudden bright sunshine, Greim walked slowly and thoughtfully to the waiting staff car, automatically returning the salutes of the orderlies marching by in the hospital's cobbled courtyard, nodding to white-coated doctors who nodded to him, thinking of the boy and telling himself that he was glad it had ended thus.

If he had lived, he would have been as terrible to see as one of the products of those 17th century *comprachicos* Conchita had told him about so long ago in the cave. For a moment or two he wondered about her and the boy. He hadn't heard from them for nearly a month, though Conchita always wrote immediately after she received the monthly sum of money he sent her from his officer's pay. But then the Spanish post was notoriously slow and the German Army's Field Post wasn't much better. Undoubtedly he'd be hearing from her soon, once the *Feldpost* caught up with the Squadron's present location.

Hardly knowing that he did so, he returned his orderly's smart salute as the man clicked to attention and opened the tourer's door for him. Colonel Greim hesitated on what he should order him to do next. There was really no need for him to return to the base. His new senior flight-commander *Major* Baron Karst was in full control. Besides they were not operational and there were no training flights scheduled for the afternoon. 'My God,' Göring had exploded, his enormous bulk wobbling like jelly, when he had first reported to him after the bombing of the bridge, 'how in three devils' name did you let them get away with it? They're all over the damned front page of every newspaper in the Reich — and that sickening, knock-kneed chicken farmer had the audacity to ring me up yesterday to tell me the Führer has ordered a whole basketful of decorations for the arrogant young swine!' He had raged for hours before commanding, 'Greim, if you value your neck, hide them, find the arsehole of the world, the deepest province — and conceal them from my sight!'

Now Greim grinned at the memory of Göring's rage. Naturally Himmler had ensured he had received new Stukas and other young SS aristocrats eager for some desperate glory, but Göring had cunningly arranged that the Squadron's fuel allowance was cut to the bare minimum. These days the First SS Stuka Squadron didn't fly much. How could they when they had hardly enough gas for their cigarette lighters?

Greim made his decision. He would forget everything and get stinking drunk this day, as he had once done in the old days back in Spain after a mission. He'd start at the Central Officers' Mess near the town's cathedral on champagne — the German Army had requisitioned huge stocks of bubbly from the local countryside. Then he'd find himself some nice discreet *bistro*, tank up on *rouge*, perhaps eat something or other, though at the moment he had never felt less like eating. Afterwards he'd visit the senior officers' brothel. Yes, he'd certainly do that. This day he needed a woman. 'Driver,' he snapped.

'Sir?'

'*Hauptkasino, bitte, und —*'

He stopped short abruptly, as Major Baron Karst's car squealed to a stop at the entrance to the hospital and the Major himself came running towards him, eye gleaming excitedly behind the monocle he affected, '*Herr Oberstleutnant!*' he cried as he ran, 'thank God I found you, sir… We're to leave at fifteen hundred hours, with or without our full Squadron strength… The rest can follow later, if necessary.'

Greim fought back his anger, knowing the answer to his question already before he posed it. 'Take a breath, Major … take a breath. What is it? Where's the fire?'

Major Karst swallowed hard and toyed with the new bauble hanging from his neck, as if he were reassuring himself that it was still there and he had really 'cured his throatache' at last. 'An urgent message from the Führer's own HQ, sir,' he blurted out. 'We've been released from the *Luftwaffe* reserve with immediate effect. General Rommel has asked for us personally and Reichsmarshal Göring has agreed to our release. I've runners out all over town rounding up the men.' Karst stared at Greim's pale craggy face, as if he couldn't believe that the older man did not share his overwhelming excitement at the tremendous news. 'Don't you understand,' he cried so that passers-by turned their heads, *we're going into action again…*'

CHAPTER 4

A pall of smoke lay over the battlefield. At the few remaining anti-tank guns, the exhausted hungry Jocks shivered. Perhaps it was due to the cool breeze coming from the Channel to their left. Perhaps it was the rumble of German tanks massing in the woods to their right. Once they would have signalled the twenty-five-pounders of the divisional artillery and they would have pounded the forest to bits. But now there were no twenty-five-pounders left. Those damned Stukas of the Germans had systematically destroyed them one by one.

The officers, as exhausted and as hungry as their men, went from position to position, telling the same old lies... 'Hundreds of reinforcements coming up... If the worst comes, the Royal Navy'll take us off tomorrow ... there'll be a hot meal for everybody this night after dark...' The bandy-legged little Jocks knew they were lies, but they nodded gravely at their officers and said, 'Ay, yer right there, sir ... I ken what yer mean.' Then they waited.

The rumble became a shudder. Red and white flares started to rise from the German start-line. Faint commands and cries floated over to the waiting Jocks. Small dark figures began to slip methodically into the corn to their front. They were coming yet once again.

'*Twenty ... twenty-five ... thirty ... thirty-five...*' the hollow-eyed anti-tank commander gave up counting helplessly. There were too many of the black-painted monsters for him. He wiped his sweaty hands on the knees of his dirty khaki pants and wished fervently for a stiff whisky.

Behind their ineffectual little guns, the Jocks tensed, holding their breath for some reason, mesmerized by the awesome sight, as the iron wave of death swept slowly towards them across the cornfield, rolling in with the power and majesty of the wild sea itself.

The young C.O.'s guts churned and yawped painfully. Now he knew why they said that somebody had the windup. He could feel physically that *he* had.

Like the roar of some infuriated beast trapped in a zoo cage, the first tank gun opened fire at the British positions. Another joined in — and another. Scarlet flashes stabbed the grey gloom. Tracer, golden-white and deadly, skimmed the heads of the corn. From the rear of the German tanks, mobile mortars thumped and thumped, their bombs screeching through space.

At last the Jocks awoke from their self-induced trance. Fear lent speed to their hands. Wheels raced round frantically. Levers were jerked. Eyes thrust against rubber eye-pieces. The first anti-tank shell went flying low and flat towards the German tanks. The white blob of solid shot struck the first one squarely on its glacis plate. Nothing happened! The German armour was too powerful for the puny British shell. It went sailing off, like a golf ball with a metallic howl.

Now the German fire started to submerge the British line. In a kind of absurd slow-motion, gun after gun was hit and rose into the burning air, scattering its crew in a welter of broken and severed limbs. Suddenly the British line began to look like the outside of some monstrous butcher's shop with human offal piled in great steaming heaps on all sides.

It was too much. Nothing seemed able to stop these inhuman monsters, grinding ever closer to the survivors. Men dropped their weapons, abandoned their positions, buried themselves into the holes, heads clutched in their hands like children trying to blot out some horrifying nightmarish noise, screaming all the while.

Officers bellowed at them. NCOs struck and kicked them. To no avail. In a matter of minutes the Germans would overrun the defensive line and already men here and there were throwing away their weapons and raising their hands in helpless surrender.

The officers gave in. 'Pull back ... *pull back everybody!*' they cried furiously, firing angrily and purposelessly at the tanks with their service revolvers, as the surviving anti-tank gunners abandoned their weapons and began to retreat across the burning fields. 'Pull back to number two position, men!'

But this terrible June day, the Germans were allowing the hard-pressed Jocks of the Fifty-First no respite. Above the fleeing men the Stukas came sweeping in like sinister black hawks from the east.

The first flight hovered above them, as if individually seeking out their prey from the fleeing brown mass below. Suddenly it peeled off, one after another. Sirens screaming hideously, engines racing all out, the gull-winged planes dropped out of the sky like black stones. Nothing seemed able to halt that death-defying dive to destruction.

The first plane came to a shuddering stop in mid-air. Its whole frame shook violently. A myriad black eggs tumbled from its blue evil belly. In a flash the air was full of the whistle of anti-personnel bombs.

The running men hadn't a chance. The bombs exploded everywhere among their fleeing ranks. Men were whirled hundreds of metres into the air. Whole groups of them disappeared in a flash. Abruptly there were dead and dying Jocks on all sides, as yet another flight peeled off. Zooming down at 400 kilometres an hour, sirens screaming, wind brakes down so that they looked like buzzards coming in for the kill, they, too, plastered the survivors with bombs.

Minutes later it was all over. Again the tanks waddled forward in the advance, churning the bodies of the anti-tank gunners to a bloody pulp beneath their flailing tracks, so that the infantry following the tanks in cautious little groups seemed to be wading through ankle-deep red slush…

The Commanding General of the 51st Highland Division, big, burly, moustached, his rumpled khaki battledress looking too small for his massive frame, lowered his glasses almost reluctantly.

He rubbed his chin and the hair rasped. All he had been able to manage this terrible morning had been a dry-shave; it hadn't been too effective. He frowned at the memory. 'Well, gentlemen,' he commenced briskly, as the German guns thundered and the seagulls swung into the wind coming over the cliffs, crying like long-lost babies, 'I won't beat about the bush.'

The staff officers knew what was coming. The Division had lost control of the country around St Valery. Now Scotland's Pride would have to fight its last battle or — But none of them was prepared to think that particularly nasty alternative to an end.

'We've lost the St Sylvain — St Valery road now. We still have the cemetery on the high ground to the rear of the port.' He gave them a faint smile. 'Hope the grave-diggers are still handy. They can bury the Boche for us, what?'

A few officers smiled, but no one laughed at the General's attempt at humour. Now they were all too exhausted for such things.

Fortune frowned and continued. 'So, there's nothing for it, but that we pull in our horns now. We simply can't stop the Hun tanks out in the open country, as you have just damned well seen.' His broad face flushed with sudden anger at the thought of how ineffective the Division's anti-tank guns had been against the German armour, like bloody pea-shooters. 'So we'll draw back into St Valery itself. There it'll be man against man, and I'm betting my Jocks will prove their match against the Boche, eh?'

There was a rumble of 'hear-hears'.

Now the German barrage was getting closer and closer and already they could hear the rusty squeak and groan of tank tracks. Suddenly General Fortune looked positively embarrassed. 'Gentlemen, let me say this before the Division's final battle commences. Undoubtedly you're asking yourselves why the Division was landed here in the first place after the main body of the British Army had already been evacuated at Dunkirk? *I* can't give you an answer. Frankly I don't know. Too, you may be asking yourselves what purpose do we serve fighting on here at St Valery? We are certainly not helping the French by doing so. The Froggies, as we have all seen, are simply falling apart.'

He licked his parched lips. Now water was being strictly rationed, and General Fortune, the most senior British soldier, left in France, had always been one to share the sufferings of his soldiers; he, too, survived on a water bottle a day.

'Again, *I* don't know, gentlemen. All I *do* know is this,' he looked around their worn, unshaven faces, iron in his voice suddenly. 'The Fifty-First Highland Division will fight like its father did in the other war — to *the end*! All right, gentlemen, start withdrawing the troops into St Valery. GOOD MORNING...'

'*Here the Royal Scots...! Over here the Gordons... Come on now, let's be having you, Headquarters Company, the Argylls... Black Watch over here. Follow me, the HLI ... KOSBs...*'

In the burning darkness, the names of those regiments and battalions which had fought the King's enemies in a dozen wars on all five continents since 1745 were yelled and bellowed, as the officers tried to regain some order, now that the dive-bombers had gone, leaving St Valery to the night and the flames.

Long lines of exhausted Jocks, bowed down under their equipment and packs so that they looked like hunchbacks, started to enter the port, the only sound their own heavy breathing and the crunch of their hobnailed boots over the broken glass which lay everywhere.

Occasionally the marching men, being directed into their new positions, caught a glimpse of a dark mysterious shadow flitting down the alleys. A looter perhaps or one of the few remaining civilians, trapped now with the soldiers. Now and then an oil dump exploded down at the docks and for a while, the long weary columns were illuminated by a bright searing flame like the sudden flash of a photographer's magnesium exploding. Then they would see the hard-faced redcaps watching them on both sides of the street, hands poised on their white-blancoed revolver holsters — significantly. There would be no deserting at St Valery.

The General, now his decision had been made for better or for worse, was everywhere, encouraging his weary Jocks, patting them on the back, handing out boiled sweets, all that he had left to give them, directing them to their positions, personally helping them to site their bren guns, assisting with the unrolling of the barbed wire.

'Got to show yer face,' he repeated over and over again to his officers as more and more infantry packed into the port and took up their last-stand positions. 'The Jocks have got to see that their officers are in the mess with them right to the end... *And their General, too!*' he added to himself sotto voce, for he knew that if he weren't killed in the battle to come, but was captured instead, it would be the end of his professional career. A mere captain could be captured and survive to become a general in some future war. But not a general. Generals did not surrender — and stay in the British Army afterwards.

This night, as General Fortune prepared his last defence, he was a very worried — and angry man, too, at the sacrifice London expected him and his Jocks to make.

Just before dawn the big heavy-set General collapsed in the striped deck-chair that bore the legend *Plage de St Valery* in the little seafront house which was now divisional headquarters. He rubbed his eyes which felt as if someone had thrown a handful of sand in them and gratefully accepted the tot of whisky, mixed with rusty-coloured water taken from the radiator of an abandoned three-tonner. 'God, I can use that, Jamie,' he breathed happily to the young aide who had brought it.

He took a sip of the mixture, ignoring the bits of rust floating in the tin mug. 'The best thing that has happened to me this long day, laddie,' he sighed. 'Like mother's milk.'

The young subaltern beamed happily. 'Good to hear it, sir. There's other good news, sir, too,' he said, keeping his surprises until the General was comfortable in his deckchair.

'Good news?' Fortune queried warily. He had not had one single piece of good news since the Division had been alerted to embark for bloody France. 'What?'

'The weather, first, sir. Listen,' like a conjuror producing a rabbit out of his top-hat, he spread his hands. On cue the first drops of rain began to splatter down on the debris-littered cobbled *pavé* outside. 'The weather forecast is that there are going to be gales out in the Channel and that means —'

'— Those ruddy Stukas won't be able to fly!' Fortune beat him to it, new hope in his lined weary face, sitting up abruptly.

'Exactly, sir. Met says that weather will be too bad for flying for the next twenty-four, perhaps even forty-eight hours.'

'Thank God for that,' Fortune said fervently. 'That will give my poor Jocks a chance to rest. My guess is that the Boche won't attack at this late stage of the game against fortified positions, risking high casualties in doing so, without that damned aerial artillery of his.' He took a sip of his mix. 'And what's the other little surprise you've got for me? You look like a cat which has just swallowed a mouse. Cough it up!'

'Well, it's a bit confused really, sir,' the young officer answered, flushing as he always did in such situations. At eighteen, as he was, he still blushed when a girl just looked at him. 'Signals are awfully bad, due to the weather out to sea, but the Divisional Signals Officer is looking into it...'

'Oh do spit it out, Jamie, please,' the General interrupted.

'It's garbled, sir,' the young officer said, face brick-red, spitting out the rest of the message in a hurry, but it seems the Navy is sending out a ship from Dover ... HMS *Drake* ... and it's heading for us ... *for St Valery!*'

Fortune looked up at the young man's excited face, his eyes full of sudden bewilderment. 'But why in heaven's name, Jamie? *Why?*'

But young Second-Lieutenant James Macpherson, who would die of hunger and typhus in a German POW camp before the year was out, had no answer to that particular overwhelming question this night.

CHAPTER 5

Outside it rained.

At first it had been a few gentle drops coming in from the Channel, soft, warm and slow, gratefully absorbed by the parched fields. But within the last hour it had become a roaring deluge. Lightning split the sky in scarlet slashes. Thunder rolled threateningly like a heavy barrage, and the rain came splashing down from the leaden sky in solid sheets.

Now cascades of water flooded the airfield. Gusts smashed against the tethered Stukas, shaking all six tons of canvas-covered metal. The grass runway was already a sea of mud. Equipment was ankle-deep in water, bombs soaked, petrol cans running with water.

But inside the tents and the huts, with the wind rattling their windows furiously, as if demanding admission, the First SS Stuka Squadron celebrated. At Reims they had 'liberated' a whole warehouse full of vintage champagne. Now they enjoyed the night, for all flying had been cancelled due to the gales expected for the next twenty-four hours. General Erwin Rommel would have to fight his last battle of the victorious campaign in France without them.

Lt. Colonel Greim had announced the news officially, while the Squadron had stood to attention in the growing gloom with the first raindrops pattering down gently. 'Soldiers of the First SS Stuka Squadron ... comrades,' he had barked, eyes sweeping their rigid ranks, the Black Knights in their handsome black leather jackets with white silk scarves, the air-gunners in the grey overalls of the *Luftwaffe* devoid of decorations, and the ground-crews in black fatigues, hands still slick with engine-grease, 'I am pleased to tell you there will be no flying for the next twenty-four hours. The whole of the Air Force in North-Eastern France has been grounded for that period of time.' He had grinned cynically, and added. 'Naturally I know you will all be very disappointed, especially you old hands of the ground crew. Anyway victory is virtually ensured. So, comrades, let us enjoy ourselves this night.' He broke out into a smile and cried the old soldier's phrase. 'Up the cups, comrades, the night will be cold! Now let's get the hell out of this shitting rain!'

So they celebrated, these young men, the veterans of the Battle of Gmünd, as they now called it, and the greenbeaks who had joined them for the great drive to the Channel Coast. Here and there a 'liberated' piano tinkled. Men sang. Others danced to gramophones, to the sad little foxtrots popular that year. But most simply got drunk, stinking drunk, for that was the quickest way to forget the war and the price of victory.

Thus it was that the gate guard almost missed the big closed grey Mercedes rattling up the water-logged, holed track, its wipers spinning back and forth furiously, trying to fight the pelting rain. Just in time a more alert sentry huddled miserably in his dripping great-coat spotted the metal flag at the top of the big gleaming bonnet. He gasped and as the car braked to a halt in a flurry of rain, cried, 'Turn out the guard … turn out the guard!'

Next moment the guard commander was at the door of the guard room, standing rigidly to attention in the yellow light that cut into the darkness, crying as if his very life depended upon it … 'General salute… For Chrissake, present arms. *Ut s General Rommel hissen!*'

Rommel slapped the raindrops from his ankle-length leather coat and tapped his peaked cap against the table, while Greim hastily poured him the glass of captured scotch whisky which he had asked for immediately the door had closed behind him. 'Absolutely filthy night, Greim,' he barked, accepting it gratefully. He raised the glass, 'And by the way congratulations on your promotion. *Prost!*'

'Thank you. *Prost Herr General!*' Greim raised his tall clouded glass of iced champagne and wondered what in heaven's name had brought out Rommel to see him on a night like this. He waited with growing apprehension, while from the mess, muted by the driving rain, there came the happy carefree laughter of the greenbeaks, being initiated into one of the Squadron's rougher games.

Rommel put down his glass and spread out his legs, little pools of water forming on the floor from his boots. 'Well, my dear Greim, you are obviously wondering what I am doing here, aren't you?' He smiled and tapped the side of his nose knowingly in the peasant fashion. 'You reason it is not customary for general officers to ride across forty kilometres of impossible French roads in this kind of weather just for a little social chat — and of course, you are right.'

'Sir,' Greim said helplessly.

Rommel held out his glass and automatically Greim poured him another drink. Outside someone was bellowing '*Wir Fahren gegen Engeland*' drunkenly, imitating the thumping of a drum by beating on what sounded like a cooking pot.

'Intelligence reported two hours ago that the British have sent a ship from Dover on the other side of the Channel — a destroyer named HMS *Drake*. Now do you know what the task of that destroyer is? I shall tell you.' Rommel took an excited drink from his glass. 'It is to pick up General Fortune and the two senior brigadiers of the 51st Highland Division so that they won't fall into my hands. Now my dear Colonel Greim, what do you conclude from that?'

Still wondering what this strange visit was about, Greim said, 'Well, I suppose, sir, it means that the British up there at St Valery are soon to surrender.'

'Exactly,' Rommel said eagerly. 'They know — if I may put it in the jargon of the common soldier — that we've got them in the pisspot and are now about to shit on them! So there is no hope for the footsloggers and they are trying now to save the brains.'

'Yes sir.'

'Now,' Rommel suddenly hesitated. Outside the drunken singing and laughter had been drowned as the rain-storm increased even more in intensity, the windows rattling furiously, the wind screaming in like a banshee. 'My attack on the 51st Highland Division will be probably the last battle to take place in the North-West, perhaps even the final battle of the whole campaign in the West, for as you know the French are on their last legs. With them it is a matter of days.'

Greim nodded.

'Undoubtedly the Tommies at St Valery will surrender in due course and it will be a great victory for the —er — Seventh Panzer Division.'

He caught himself just in time and Greim told himself he had meant 'great victory for General Erwin Rommel.' He said nothing, however.

'But the fall of St Valery and the surrender of the Tommies would be an even greater victory if I managed to capture General Fortune. So far not one single German commander has managed to capture a British general officer. We've had Dutch generals, Belgian generals, French generals, even

Luxembourger generals, if such officers exist,' he chuckled, 'but *never* a British one. At Dunkirk they carefully removed them, Alexander, Alanbrooke, Montgomery and all the rest, though God knows what they intend to do with them, now that they have lost the war. Now my dear Greim, I want to capture Fortune. *His* misfortune, if I may make a pun, would be *my* fortune. You know what the Führer and Dr Goebbels would make of it?'

'Yes, I understand that, sir. But what has it got to do with me?' Greim asked, puzzled.

'This. I want this Tommy ship — this HMS *Drake* — destroyed before it ever reaches St Valery. It is the only way that I can capture Fortune. Yes, yes,' he held up his hand to stop Greim speaking, 'I know what you are going to say. Why can't the *Kriegsmarine* deal with the Tommy ship once it has picked up the Tommy general. But that isn't the same, you see. Then the *Kriegsmarine* would get whatever honour that was going, not me … and naturally my division.' The ambition blazed in full naked fury from the Swabian general's eyes. There was no mistaking it.

'But sir,' Greim objected, pointing to the door which rattled violently, the wind sweeping underneath it and lifting up the edges of the shabby, threadbare carpet. 'Listen to that. Do you know what you are asking me to do — *in that kind of weather!*' A sudden rage overcame him. '*Himmelherrgott!*' he exploded, 'don't you know that the whole of the German *Luftwaffe* is grounded due to the terrible weather conditions! It is virtually impossible to fly in this weather.'

'But not for the First SS Stuka Squadron, Greim,' Rommel said quite mildly. His eyes narrowed cunningly. 'Your young hotheads would go with or *without* your permission, you know,

Greim. They all believe in the old motto — to get on, you have to go along with.'

Greim sank back in his chair. Outside the wind howled mournfully. He knew Rommel was right; his Black Knights would do exactly as Rommel had said.

'Göring would object,' he tried.

Rommel shrugged carelessly. 'Reichsmarshal Göring is an important man, Greim, but his star is sinking. I have the backing of Himmler, and who has the Führer's ear these days? ... *Himmler.*'

Greim knew he was beaten. 'All right, sir,' he said, voice low and depressed, 'but you know it could well mean the end of the First SS Stuka Squadron.'

Rommel reached for his cap. He was unmoved. 'Germany is full of young eager men who would take their place, Greim... Your Black Knights are expendable...'

With that General Rommel was gone, hurrying out into the beating rain.

CHAPTER 6

Tractors rumbled through the mud dragging up the two thousand pound bombs, one for each Stuka. Bowsers pumped the planes full of gas. Armourers fed in long belts of ammunition, their overalls soaked with rain, and all the while the storm raged, the wind howling in straight from the sea, cold and furious.

In the Ops Room the intelligence NCOs worked under the swaying yellow light of the naked bulbs, making sure that each pilot's wallet contained a complete set of maps and photographs for identification purposes; while standing on a ladder, a corporal fixed a long ribbon across the blue of the Channel on the map, indicating the route the Stukas would take.

Behind, the pilots and gunners began to assemble. Now there was no sign of the previous evening's high spirits. Their intent young faces seemed ageless now like the faces of men who were going to face death — and knew it. They flashed glances at the big map and waited. Outside the rain beat and rattled at the windows, the raindrops streaming down the glass like cold, sad tears.

Colonel Greim came in. He, too, was in flying gear. Major Karst, who wasn't, surprisingly, barked angrily, '*Stillgestanden!*' They clicked to attention and Greim touched his hand to his battered cap casually, 'Stand at ease, please, gentlemen.' He mounted the platform at the end of the room and faced them, feeling as always when he had performed this little ceremony that he had entered another world.

'I shall make it brief. You know our mission. It's going to be tricky to find a single ship in the middle of the Channel especially in this weather. So we'll fly in formation, sections of four, line abreast — and don't straggle or you'll certainly lose contact in this lousy visibility. Absolute R/T silence of course until we make contact. If you can, use only visual signals.'

Greim took a breath. 'The attack formation. Tiger,' he nodded to de la Mazière who commanded Tiger Flight, 'you will go in first.'

De la Mazière inclined his head to acknowledge he had understood, but also to hide the look of joy in his eyes. The Old Man was giving him the opportunity to cure his throatache at last! He'd get first crack at the target at a time when the flak would be lightest.

'You next, Panther,' he looked at Hanno van Heiter who was holding on tightly to his dog, his knuckles white, face intent. 'Or should we call your flight Fiffi — after that absurd pooch of yours?' He smiled and Hanno von Heiter managed to return it.

'Jaguar will come in third,' he looked at Freiherr von Krings, a tall very blond officer who had come to replace Schwarz. The Freiherr returned his look proudly.

Greim paused and then let them have it. 'I shall take Lion myself, coming in last.'

There was a gasp of surprise. Karst, who already had been told that he wasn't flying this day, glared angrily out of the window at the streaming rain. Hanneman nudged Slack Arse significantly and grinned in spite of one hell of a hangover that no amount of oxygen from the cylinder seemed to be able to cure. Slack Arse grinned back. They knew why Karst had been grounded this day to be replaced by the Colonel. The Old Man wanted no heroics this morning, which might endanger the whole Squadron; he was going to take charge of the bombing himself.

Almost as if he had read the grinning NCO's mind, Greim said, 'This might well be our last mission of the war, comrades. There is talk that England will surrender soon. So,' he emphasized the word, 'I want no foolishness. No unnecessary waste of life. I want you to press your attack to the utmost, but I do *not* want you to take absurd risks. Any questions?'

There were none. 'All right. That's all.' Greim took one last look at their young faces. 'Good luck ... and good hunting!'

'*Stillgestanden!*' Karst barked.

Greim saluted and was gone.

The white flare swept up from the make-shift control tower, blazing and spluttering furiously as it rose through the rain. De la Mazière opened the throttle. His Stukas did the same. Two abreast they began to roll forward through the mud, the rain beating angrily against each canopy. Mud splattered up high. Next to de la Mazière the other Stuka veered sharply to the left. De la Mazière groaned. It was one of the greenbeaks. He was off the track altogether. The fool was opening his throttle even wider. Mud shot up in a thick brown goo, his wheels sinking ever deeper. Then he was stuck altogether.

'Number Four's gone off, sir,' Slack Arse reported, 'Arse over tip, but I don't think anybody's hurt.'

'*Scheisse!*' de la Mazière cursed, as his Stuka started to rise at last into the pouring rain, 'now the clock's really in the bucket! Half the shitting flight aborted even before we start the mission!'

If the fact that in the end only ten aircraft succeeded in taking off in those terrible conditions worried de la Mazière, it didn't Colonel Greim. Flying through the rain like a ghostly school of porpoises, keeping together just above the first green swell of the Channel below, Greim was pleased at that figure. At least six of his young pilots and their gunners would be saved now — and he was going to do his damned best to save the rest. Arrogant and ambitious as they were, he was not going to throw away the lives of his Black Knights — or the peasants, too, for that matter — just to further General Erwin Rommel's career. They'd find the Tommy destroyer, if they could, and attack, too; but it would be one attack-dive per Stuka — that had been the reason he had personally decided on the one single 2000 lb bomb — and then away into the cover of the storm. 'Don't worry, Conchita and Miguel,' he said to himself — for these days, lonely man that he was, he found himself often talking to them — 'I'll bring the young hotheads back. Myself, too, *hasta luego*.' Then waggling his wings in signal, he started to climb, the others following, entering that wild opaque moving wall.

Below the ground crew stared up silently into the murk, listening to the sound of the engines die away, watching the straight swathes of white etched on the grey by the burning exhaust gases slowly begin to disappear. The Black Knights were on their way...

Down in the heaving bowels of the *Drake*, the engines pumping away steadily in spite of the monstrous sea like the beat of a heart, the rating stared hypnotically at the green swing of the glowing needle as it covered its 360 degree arc.

The destroyer was four hours out of Dover now and it should have long since reached St Valery, but in spite of the weather the skipper had insisted on a complicated zig-zag course in order to fool any lurking E-boat. Now finally he was beginning to steer for port, obviously confident that not even the *Kriegsmarine* would venture out in weather like this, the destroyer's knife-like prow hitting every new line of waves as if slamming into a brick wall.

The interference was terrible, the rating told himself, as he watched the jerking oscilloscope. The weather up top must be ruddy horrible. It was so bad that it was hardly worth watching.

The Leading Hand seemed to think the same. He staggered over to the Rating crouched over his instrument in the semi-gloom of the radar shack and said, 'Give it a rest, Chalkey. Yer'll go dolalli trying to make sense of that mess... They say there's snorkers for tea — 'He stopped short. 'Hey, Chalkey, look at that!' A very faint blip had appeared on the extreme edge of the round screen, right on top. Automatically the Leading Hand called out the bearing, 'Three, thirty degrees!'

Hastily Chalkey turned his dials and knobs. The blip seemed to be zig zagging slowly, coming back on itself and then going north again. There seemed no method to it.

For five long minutes the two sailors watched it, while the destroyer cut through the pounding heavy seas, getting ever closer to St Valery; then it vanished, leaving them staring at a screen empty of anything save interference. Chalkey looked at the Leading Hand, puzzled. 'Well, what do you think, Taffy?' he asked, easing his headphones from his ears and wiping the sweat from them. 'Search me, mate,' the other man answered. 'But log it just in case.' He sniffed, 'Nobody in his right mind would be out on a ruddy night like this... Come on, close her up for tea. Let's get one of them snorkers before those greedy buggers from the engine-room grab 'em all.'

Together the two seamen staggered out of the shack to eat their sausage, lying in a pool of grease, to be dipped up by hunks of stale bread. It would be the last meal they would ever eat.

'Holy strawsack, sir,' Slack Arse Schmidt cursed, as they entered the sheer black wall of the new gale, 'this is really something for the book!' He choked, as the Stuka was buffeted by the great wind and lightning zig-zagged alarmingly, cutting the cloud for an instant with a vicious purple bolt of light.

'Don't talk,' de la Mazière snapped through tight lips, hanging onto the controls grimly, 'keep your eyes on my number two. Don't want that greenbeak ramming me in this mess.'

'He's gone, sir,' Slack Arse answered. 'Went a minute ago.'

'Why didn't —' de la Mazière gave up. It wasn't worth getting angry about. Now it was every man for himself. He concentrated on flying.

Now it was pitch-black all around him. Rain poured into the cockpit. Fierce gusts of wind shook and rattled the aircraft. Despite the roar of the engine, he could hear the hellish howl of the wind and the crash of thunder.

His eye fell for an instant on his rectangular instrument panel. He gasped. Something was wrong. The needle of the vertical speed indicator had ceased to oscillate, and next to it, the air speed indicator was accelerating alarmingly with every second. He flashed a look at the altimeter, the only instrument which could give some clue to what was happening to the Stuka. His eyes opened wide. *They were falling rapidly!*

The ASI started to register an ever increasing speed. Two hundred kilometres an hour ... two hundred fifty ... three hundred kilometres ... four hundred!

Behind him Slack Arse Schmidt held on to his seat with both hands like a child about to be thrown off a wildly rocking roundabout. De la Mazière almost panicked. For some unknown reason the Stuka was racing down through the wall of darkness at an impossible speed in an almost perpendicular dive.

He began to sweat, as he fought the controls. The liquid poured off him. The altimeter was falling by the instant. At this rate he'd slam right into the sea in a matter of seconds. Cursing furiously, he tugged and slapped, trying to regain control. Now they were down to one thousand metres. Some of the instruments were swinging back into place. But the stick was shuddering frighteningly.

Down and down they hurtled to their doom. Lightning stabbed the darkness on both sides. It was as if they were diving through a black tunnel. With both hands, his feet braced against the floor, his shoulder muscles burning with blazing agony, he heaved at the stick. In a minute it would be too late. He was down to five hundred metres.

Blood pounded at his temples. He choked for breath. His eardrums popped and bubbled, as if they would burst at any moment. Thick black blood spurted from his distended nostrils. A gigantic hand squeezed his face flat.

A thump. A groan. He heaved again with the last of his strength. The stick started to come back, moaning and whining like a live thing at this intolerable strain. Every rivet squealed. The Stuka shuddered. For a moment de la Mazière, pressed hard against the back of his seat, his intestines seeming to thrust against his spine, blacked out. And then Slack Arse Schmidt was screaming hysterically behind him. 'It's the Tommy, sir ... the *Tommy*!'

De la Mazière shook his head to clear the black mist away and flashed a look downwards.

There it was sliding through the green heaving, whitecapped sea like a grey shark, two foaming white curves of spray combing from the sharp prow. There was no mistaking the silhouette of a Tommy Afridi-class destroyer.

De la Mazière did not hesitate. 'To all,' he barked into his mike, 'Tiger One here. I've found her... Going into the attack. *ENDE!*'

Greim came racing in at wave-top height. It was the only way to escape the raging storm. Now the grey mass was rolling to his front, looking ever larger as it came out of the rain. Squat funnels, raised gun platform, a tangle of wires and aerials. It was the *Drake* all right and already she had spotted the black hawks hovering all about her in the whirling sky, ready to pounce at any moment. Clusters of red and green tracer were spurting in every direction and her four-inch guns were being elevated desperately to tackle the attackers.

Instinctively Greim ducked as salt water blurred his windscreen, telling himself that his original plan was no good. His Stuka pilots, carried away by their patriotism and overweening ambition, would attack in any order. He had to protect them the best he could. He pressed the bomb toggle. The great two thousand pound bomb plunged harmlessly into the sea and the Stuka, lightened, raced forward into the mêlée. 'Hanneman, you rogue, there's seven days' leave in Berlin for this,' he gasped, as 20mm shells began to explode all about them. 'We've got to give the young fools some sort of chance, if we can.'

What do you want to do, sir?' Hanneman yelled.

'Strafe the gunners the best you can,' he screamed above the terrible chatter of the massed pom-poms on the destroyer's deck. 'Use your m.g. I'm coming in broadsides.'

Hurriedly Hanneman swung his gun round.

'*Here we go!*'

Greim swung the plane round in a tight turn. Giving the Stuka full throttle, he came zooming in out of the rain and black cloud. All hell erupted on the destroyer's deck. He seemed to be racing by a solid wall of fire. Every gun on the ship was directed at him. Puffballs of smoke exploded on all sides. The Stuka shuddered violently time and time again.

Behind him Hanneman pumped long furious bursts, finger hard down on the button. His tracer ripped the length of the destroyer above the waterline and raced upwards up the hull towards the rails. A wind-scoop came crashing down. Steam suddenly spurted from somewhere. Two men in blue flung themselves to the deck and the tracer ripped their backs apart as they lay there. He could see the sudden blood-red button holes appear the length of their backs. Then they were soaring past the ship, the flak chasing them as they disappeared into the cloud already trailing black smoke behind them.

A Stuka missed them by metres — a great hurtling black shape, which set Greim's plane rocking violently so that he had to hold the stick in both hands. Next instant the other Stuka had plunged engine-first into the waves and a huge spout of whirling white water erupted.

'Von Krings, I think,' Hanneman said grimly, as Greim tore round to come in again. 'Those greenbeaks don't have a chance ... poor shits!'

Greim said nothing. He came in again, skimming the green heaving surface of the water, going flat out.

Again the *Drake* loomed up out of the storm, looking like a floating fortress, all guns blazing. The air was crisscrossed with multi-coloured tracer. Shells exploded everywhere. The sky was full of black and white puffs of smoke.

Greim gritted his teeth again as he prepared to run the gauntlet once more. To port two Stukas appeared suddenly, coming from separate angles. *Break ... for God's sake, break!*' he screamed, knowing what would happen. Too late! The planes slammed into each other. A great rending crash. A blaze of fire. Shredded metal came racing their way like flak. Behind him Hanneman's machinegun began to chatter once more. White tracer zipped towards the destroyer's gun deck. A loader went down with infinite slowness, still cradling the gleaming yellow shell to his broad chest, as if it were some precious baby, as he sank to the deck. A tumble of steel rigging fell, trailing furious red sparks behind it. Suddenly the crazed Colonel saw the banked machine-guns. He knew the British called them 'Chicago pianos'. Now they seemed all to be pointing right at him.

They were. He broke violently. Too late. A burst of 50-inch shells ricocheted off his hood. Stars appeared suddenly all over the splintered opaque wall which had abruptly blinded him. A stream of oil began to spread over it. He rolled the aircraft over on its back, the only tactic he could think of. A keen blast of wind blew in through the canopy. It would clear the glass and the oil.

Now he was flying parallel with the ship at fifty metres above the waves. For a moment he was too surprised or paralysed to do anything, not even worried about the tracer which was beginning to home in on the Stuka once more.

Hanneman's frantic yell woke him to his danger. 'Get up, sir!... *For God's sake, get up...*'

He kicked the rudder and jerked the stick. The violence of the manoeuvre almost caught him off guard. The black veil started to spread over his vision once again. He shook his head, scattering beads of sweat all over the shattered cockpit. He was climbing again at a tremendous rate. The destroyer started to fall back behind him. Now it was almost toylike. He was doing it. He was going to make it!

The crump of the flak shell hitting the cockpit caught him totally and completely by surprise. The shock was so great that he emptied his bowels there and then, something he had never done in combat before. Suddenly everything was damp, warm and soggy. But not only below the belt. His face had a strange wet glutinous feel about it. Even as Lt. Colonel Greim reached out one hesitant gloved hand to feel his cheek and ascertain the damage, he knew with the absolute, overwhelming clarity of a vision that Conchita's *comprachicos* had got him at last…

Hanno von Heiter held on to the stick, as if his very life depended upon it. Down below, glimpsed through a gap in the scudding black clouds and the furious gusts of rain, there it was — the British warship. Its whole deck seemed alive with cherry-coloured flame. Shells were screaming out from its guns at every angle. Tracer filled the air with its lethal morse. And to port, the C.O.'s plane was limping away, trailing thick black smoke behind it.

He gulped, feeling the hot bitter bile rising in his throat. There was no denying it. He was afraid. How could he bring himself to fling the plane down right into the middle of that awesome flak? He wouldn't — he *couldn't* — survive! Cold damp beads of sweat broke out on his forehead. What was he going to do? '*Los, Mensch*,' that same cunning voice that had plagued him ever since that raid on the bridge at Gmünd urged, 'Get out of it while there's still time. In this weather anyone could be excused for not finding the target. Abort the mission. No one will ever know!'

The gunner will, he told himself, fighting to retain control of himself. Oh, yes he will! Then there would be the sly little tales in the peasants' mess and soon the ground crew would be casting knowing glances at him when they thought he wasn't looking. Finally it would reach the Black Knights. Karst would cut him dead. De la Mazière would try to understand, but would fail; brave men such as de la Mazière cannot understand cowardice. Finally he would be asked to see the C.O. The Old Man would be kind, but would recommend he should go. They'd find some sort of medical excuse. A ruptured intestine, something wrong with his aorta, that sort of thing: dive-bomber pilots were always being afflicted by mysterious complaints, due to the pressure of the dive.

He'd be sent home on half-pay to be confronted by his father — the General. There would be pointed questions with his father glaring at him from below those impressive white eyebrows. Excuses, half-truths wouldn't put him off. In the end he'd break down and confess he was a coward. There'd be talk of shame, the honour of the family, the disgrace, and in the end he'd find that little pistol in the study one evening when the General had retired and the brief note in his father's old-fashioned Gothic scrawl, ordering him to 'take a gentleman's way out'.

Suddenly von Heiter thrust the stick forward. The Stuka's nose dipped immediately. He increased the angle of the dive. Sixty degrees … seventy… Now he was falling out of the sky at eighty degrees. The destroyer started to fill the whole of the gap in the clouds. He was sliding down a black tunnel towards the *Drake*. He retracted his air brakes. His speed increased enormously. The gunners spotted him. Angry red flashes spurted from below. Puffballs of smoke erupted on all sides. The Stuka shuddered. He could hear the shrapnel striking his wings and howling off in ricochets. The *Drake* was centred plumb in the middle of his sights. The ship fascinated him. He couldn't seem to break away. Slowly his thumb sought the bomb release switch on the stick. Below the sailors were scattering furiously, dropping flat on the debris-littered deck. Still he could not break the spell the ship had for him. Behind him his gunner was shrieking, '*Break, sir ... break sir... FOR GOD'S SAKE ... BRE—AK!*' On and on he hurtled in that suicidal dive, as if he wanted it to end thus, get the messy business of living, the sham of it all, over with once and for all. Now he was well below the height for dropping the 2000 lb bomb. The fragmentation effect reached 1,000 metres and he was two hundred below that.

CRUMP! The Stuka shuddered terribly. His cockpit was filled with the acrid stink of burnt explosive. Instinctively he pressed the button. The Stuka gave a huge leap. He tugged back the stick with all his strength. For a moment he saw nothing. A black veil slid before his eyes, bulging wild like those of a madman, his mouth wide open gasping for breath and then his gunner was yelling wildly, 'She's stopping, sir ... she's stopping, sir... *We must have hit her...*'

De la Mazière braced himself. A thousand metres below, he could catch glimpses of the *Drake* drifting helplessly, oil leaking from her port side and calming the waves that battered her now that she had lost power. Hanno's bomb must have put her engines out of commission, he told himself, but her flak was still firing. Already what looked like a string of glowing coals was rippling towards him. Suddenly bright angry lights flashed all around him. Instinctively he opened the throttle wide and climbing, hanging on to his prop, raced for the protection of another lowering black storm cloud.

'Are we going to abort, sir?' Slack Arse Schmidt cried above the howling motor, a look of hope on his pale face. 'That tin can's had it. The sailor boys can finish her off with torpedoes when this storm blows out. No use risking our lives, is it?' De la Mazière hesitated. He knew the air gunner was right. The *Drake* was finished. At all events she would never be able to reach St Valery now and carry out her rescue mission. General Fortune was as good as in the bag already. Yet, should he just fly away? He felt his neck instinctively. That precious black and white cross was not yet hanging there. He had still not cured his throatache. 'No,' he said firmly, 'hold on to your hat, Schmidt, we're going in for the attack!'

Boldly he broke out of the cloud once more. Clusters of tracer raced up to meet him at once. Shells burst to left and right. He went into the dive. A ring of fine white puffs made by 20mm shells formed to his front. He raced straight through them. His acceleration, weighed down as the Stuka was with that 2000 pounds of high explosive, was terrific. Within seconds the crippled destroyer, its superstructure riddled with holes, wireless masts trailing in the water, filled his sight enormously.

Bang! ... Bang! He held onto the control stick desperately. The Stuka trembled like a wild animal under the impact. Shrapnel screamed through the aluminium plates. His nostrils were assailed by the stink of hot metal, cordite, burnt rubber. Suddenly de la Mazière was sick with fear. This was the end, he knew it. He'd had it! Still he did not break off his attack. He continued to hurtle out of the sky into that deadly maelstrom of flying metal. Blood thumped in his right leg. His toes were curled up in a glutinuous mess. He had been wounded. He raced on. White tracer filled the sky in a solid wall. Ricochets howled off hysterically. Fist-sized fragments of shells pounded the Stuka, but still he didn't pull her out of that death-defying dive.

'*NOW!*' he screamed.

His thumb hit the button. The plane leapt, as the great bomb sprang from the bomb-bay. Fascinated, still diving, de la Mazière watched it fall. He knew he couldn't miss. And he didn't.

Two thousand pounds of high explosive slammed into the *Drake* amidships. The noise of the explosion, followed immediately by the rending screech of tearing metal, drowned even the thunder of the guns. Steam started to escape at once. A huge white jet of it hissed out of the companionways and spurted upwards. De la Mazière stared at it incredulously as it raced towards the Stuka. He seemed unable to move, brake, do anything, his whole being frozen by the shocking sight; then his plane was rocked and tossed from side to side by the rising turbulence, the paint bubbling suddenly on its plates as the boiling hot steam struck, and de la Mazière acted...

'They'll make it, if they're lucky, sir,' Slack Arse Schmidt said, voice low, deliberately kept unemotional, expressing no sense of triumph at their great victory, as the last of the little boats pulled away from the dying ship, below.

'I hope so,' de la Mazière said, his voice low, too, as he took in that final terrible spectacle.

Now the *Drake*, her superstructure trailing in the oil-scum that surrounded her, her white ensign still flying proudly, readied herself to go under. She shuddered violently, as yet another ammo store exploded. Red flame seared her body-littered grey steel deck in a huge blowtorch of fire. Her bow blew off. For a fleeting moment, her stern reared high into the black storm-ridden sky, propellers spinning, that proud white tattered flag stiff in the breeze. Suddenly she reeled, shuddered. A terrible groaning, an eerie keening came from her that could be heard two hundred metres up in the steadily circling lone plane. Desperately the survivors bent and strained at their oars, knowing what was coming, trying to get away while there was still time.

One second later, her oil tanks exploded. The Stuka rocked violently under the impact of that explosion. De la Mazière choked. It felt as if a giant hand had just squeezed his guts. He gasped for breath like a stranded fish. A monstrous funeral pyre of flame shot into the sky. The *Drake* began to slide under rapidly. The green heaving water leapt up to receive her. Next instant the waves seemed to recoil, hissing and spluttering furiously, as they felt the searing heat of the red-hot plates. Not for long. In one final wild tumult of whirling white water, she was gone, leaving behind her a shocked awed silence and the little black boats rocking helplessly in the huge wave that signalled her end.

Unconsciously de la Mazière raised his hand to his flying helmet as if in salute, then tugged at the stick. 'Let's go home, Schmidt,' he said wearily, 'it's all over now.' He opened the throttle. Behind them and below, the men in the little boats disappeared, left to the mercy of the sea and, if they survived, to the long bitter years to come…

ENVOI

It was '*Führerwetter*'.

A perfect blue sky. Sparkling summer sunshine. A soft warm breeze. Rarely did this northern city experience anything like it. Today, the Gods smiled on Germany.

Berlin, the capital, sparkled in the sun. Everywhere the outdoor cafes and restaurants that lined the capital's streets were packed with well-dressed women in hats and veils talking animatedly over champagne and strawberries to elegant, attentive, young bronzed officers proudly sporting their new decorations. Flags flew bravely everywhere. Flowers hung in baskets from the lampposts. Soldiers in pairs strode back and forth in their pressed uniforms and gleaming boots, in step, slapping up a tremendous salute every time they saw an officer. On all sides military greetings were barked to and fro. Civilians clicked out their right arms every few metres and cried 'Heil Hitler' fervently. Somewhere an Army band played, all crashing cymbals and blaring brass. This wonderful summer's day, the very air of Berlin seemed heavy with victory.

The tall walls of the courtyard of the splendid new Reichs-Chancellery, designed by Speer himself, muted the noise a little. Here in the shade cast by the building, it was pleasantly cool, for which the men waiting there excitedly were grateful. It was not every day that one met the Führer. Most of them were already sweating in anticipation as it was.

'All right, sir?' Sergeant Hanneman, erect and smart in a brand new *Luftwaffe* uniform, complete with decorations, asked.

Colonel Greim, sitting in his bathchair, the side of his face still swathed in bandages, grinned the best he could ... the graft Sauerbruch, the famous surgeon, had ordered for the left side of his terribly wounded face was very taut. 'Why shouldn't I be all right, you big rogue?' he answered. 'I've got the big one haven't I?' He indicated the new Knight's Cross dangling from his neck, 'have pretty nurses half my age fussing over me all day long ... you'd give your right arm to get the kind of bed-bath they give me ... and I've got a great horned-ox of a hairy-assed noncom like yourself to push me around in this crate. What else do I want?'

He might have added Conchita and Miguel, but he didn't. He knew that wasn't to be now. Conchita must never see him as a victim of the *comprachicos*, but at least they were well and happy. He had read and re-read the letter he had received from her this morning a dozen times already.

Hanneman grinned and nudged Slack Arse happily, nodding at the C.O.'s greying head. It was good to see the Old Man in such good form again. Pill, the Squadron sawbones, had told him confidentially that Sauerbruch had told him, Pill, that the Old Man would be flying again within three months, though he would be disfigured for life. That had been a relief. He would have hated to know that Major *shitting* Baron *shitting* Karst would take over the Squadron.

Greim looked across at his Black Knights, every one of the flight commanders now sporting the 'cure' for their throatache proudly. How handsome and dashing they looked in their black leather tunics, white silk scarves and gleaming topboots, their peaked caps set at a jaunty, rakish angle, even Karst's! He nodded his approval. Arrogant bastards they might be, he told himself, but now after France they were the *Luftwaffe's* best dive-bomber pilots. Even Fat Hermann, his old friend Göring, had to admit that. They were the élite. There were none better. He caught de la Mazière's eye and the tall young pilot with the bronzed open face smiled back at him. How happy and gay he looked this beautiful summer afternoon; yet a couple of times when he had returned to the mess from the hospital to visit his Squadron, he caught the youngster off guard, alone in the darkening mess, half-touched drink in his hand, staring out at the empty parade ground, face set and unrevealing. *Thinking?* About what? he had wondered.

But whatever the young officer's problem might be, today he had dismissed it from his mind. He was as excited and as enthusiastic as the rest. Even Karst showed just how overwrought he was; for he was constantly taking out that absurd monocle of his and screwing it back in his eye with an exaggerated contortion of his jaw and facial muscles.

'*Habt acht!*' the harsh bark of the SS sergeant-major's command cut into Colonel Greim's reveries.

'*Stillgestanden!*' the massive black-clad noncom rasped.

The giants with their white cross-belts stamped attention.

The kettledrummer rattled his little drum.

'*Present arms!*' the command echoed and re-echoed throughout the shady courtyard.

There were three perfect, simultaneous slaps as hard hands hit the rifles, and there he was, the Führer, Adolf Hitler, the Leader of the new Reich which was going to last 1,000 years. Proudly he walked the length of the SS guard of honour, arm raised parallel with his shoulder, as the giants' heads followed him, as if worked by springs. At the end of the honour-guard, he paused, clicked his heels together, and gave that flag which now flew victoriously from the Vistula to the Channel Coast the full-arm salute.

Greim nodded to a waiting Karst. The Major knew his duty. He snapped to attention and bellowed. '*Offiziere des ersten* SS *Stuka Geschwaders* — *STILLGESTANDEN!'*

As one the Black Knights clicked to attention, faces tense with emotion, eyes burning, as Karst took three paces forward and bellowed, *'Mein Führer,* I beg to report the officers of the First SS Stuka Squadron — *present and correct!'* Towering above the Leader, he flung up his right arm in the German greeting. Hitler flapped back his own arm and for one long moment his dark eyes swept from one face to another, fixing each pilot with that hypnotic look of his, as if he were trying to burn their features into his mind's eye for eternity.

'Comrades ... soldiers of the German Air Force!' he cried, that tremendous hoarse Upper Austrian voice reverberating back and forth across the courtyard, sending the pigeons rising in soft, fluttering protest from the flat roof. 'You have fought well. Each and every one of you. I pay my humble respects to your devotion to duty — to your sacrifice, your idealism, your belief in the National Socialist cause. You and you alone have helped Germany to achieve a tremendous victory!'

De la Mazière felt that hypnotic gaze burn right into the core of his very being. At that tremendous moment, he knew he could never betray this man. His doubts of these last few weeks vanished, as if they had never existed. The man standing before them could never do anything wrong; he knew that implicitly as an article of faith. Adolf Hitler was a good man, whose very life was Germany. He felt a wave of almost overwhelming pride surge through his blood. At that moment he felt drunk with excitement and loyalty.

'There is still *one* enemy left!' Hitler cried. With an impatient and characteristic jerk of his head, he threw back that black lock of hair which threatened to fall into his burning eyes and thrust up his cleft pugnacious jaw as if he were challenging the

Gods themselves to dare prevent him from achieving his destiny. 'Perfidious Albion!

But that drunken sot Churchill will not stop the New Germany. The decadent British Empire cannot halt the march of the New Order. In due course it will fall apart and *then* we will have final victory!'

He paused dramatically and stared at their young fanatical faces with those burning madman's eyes of his, his chest heaving with the effort of speaking.

For one fleeting second, a cloud appeared from somewhere, marring that perfect sky. A shadow crossed the faces of his listeners. They vanished into the darkness, standing there like black ghosts, motionless and waiting. But for what? Then the shadow was gone, as if it had never been there. Greim swallowed hard, but the vision of death had vanished. His Black Knights were back again, young, vital, full of burning fervour and devotion to the man who stood before them.

'There will be battles in the future, comrades,' Hitler shrieked, his face suddenly furious with rage. 'Those decadents across the Channel, spurred on by the machinations of international Jewish capital, will continue the fight! But victory will be ours, never fear!' He wagged a finger at them like a schoolmaster lecturing his pupils, the rage vanishing as quickly as it had appeared, 'And you, dear comrades, will win that fight.' His face softened and his voice sank to almost a whisper. 'For you are the élite of the élite.'

De la Mazière flushed with pride. At that moment the Führer seemed to be looking directly at him. How wise, how proud, how all-knowing those dark burning eyes seemed — like those of some great father!

Hitler clicked to attention, his speech finished. *'My Knights of the Iron Cross — I salute ye!'* he rasped, flinging up his arm.

'*SIEG HEIL!*' Karst cried, carried away by an overwhelming sublime emotion.

'*SIEG HEIL!*' those hoarse enthusiastic voices roared exultantly. Dead on cue, as planned, as that triumphant cry echoed back and forth across the courtyard, the lone plane came racing in. All eyes swung to the heavens.

Like a sinister black hawk it hovered there abruptly in the burning blue sky, all-conquering and infinitely evil: the symbol of the might of this New Germany in the year of victory 1940 … *THE STUKA…*

A NOTE TO THE READER

Dear Reader,

If you have enjoyed this novel enough to leave a review on **Amazon** and **Goodreads**, then we would be truly grateful.

Sapere Books

.

Sapere Books is an exciting new publisher of brilliant fiction and popular history.

To find out more about our latest releases and our monthly bargain books visit our website:
saperebooks.com

Printed in Great Britain
by Amazon